"I enjoyed it. When I first read it, I
What started out looking like just a:
be a well thought out, well writt
powerful young men."

- *Reginald Fields*

"Good read. Deals with real-life issues of the day. Good plot, makes you think and want more. A must-read!"

- *Michael Gutekunst*

"Compelling. Good vocabulary. Well-written. Great syntax. Page turner!"

- *Carlos Goodman*

"A work of fiction that calls attention to a long-standing non-fiction social issue."

- *Joseph Marcy*

"That jawn definitely mean. I like how the different stories were tied in. The content was on point. I like how it matches today. Above average. Unexpected. I wanted more, but I guess that's a good thing."

- *Dwayne Washington*

"That jawn hot! It was a good read! It was a good read! *Hero or Criminal* was a very interesting read, with its well thought out story line; which included real-life and believable scenarios... It kept me on the edge wanting to skip ahead to see how things turned out. It was by far one of the best fiction books I've read in a long time. Thank you... "

- *Alex Crespo*

"The book was a really good read. I genuinely felt in suspense the entire book... I read it overnight at work last weekend in one sitting."

- Cameron Strong

"It reads good. It's easy to follow along. A very good read with real-life scenarios. Although a work of fiction, in these days this could very well be a true story. Good job man! I liked it!"

- Duane Jones

"Wow. Very real... You have my vote! Truthfully, I don't have enough space to express everything I can say. Kudos. It was good man. Very well written. It's so vivid. Whoever went through a similar ordeal, they gonna have aftershocks. As a person fighting for their life, I couldn't help but to have moments reading this book where I could feel emotions. I can remember getting shot. It reads like a movie. Even though I'm not from there, I can see it all. It's a very vivid read. It's a page-turner! Hats off to you."

- Terrence Graham

Colin Patterson

NWP

Narrow Way Publishers

Philadelphia, PA 19153

Designed by Narrow Way Collective

Manufactured in the United States of America

ISBN 979-8-218-04302-5

www.narrowwaypublishers.com

To Mom, for so much.

"The next move that you make could be your last." – Martseah Ehbed

PROLOGUE

*T*HE HEAVILY TATTOOED Haitian looked like he should have been in a strongman competition instead of a prison. With boulder-sized biceps, triceps, pecs, and delts threatening to rip his T-shirt to shreds; and muscular thighs thinking of doing the same thing to his brown trousers; there was absolutely no need for him to have a weapon. Nine times out of ten, just *one* of the massive man's punches was all that it took.

But since restraint had never been one of his strong suits, the behemoth crept toward the end of the cinderblock wall, holding a crudely-fashioned knife in his hand, the blade resting against the inside of his forearm and pointed up at his armpit, his arm pressed close to his body.

He could hear his target making scuffing noises right around the corner—probably loading a wooden pallet with boxes full of finished product.

If the Haitian timed his assault right, the blade would be buried deep in Terrell Jackson's spine before he even knew what hit him. The knife wielding giant peeked around the wall and liked his odds. He took a deep breath and planted the ball of his Reebok-clad foot into the unfinished concrete floor, taking off at a dead sprint. His big size fifteens quickly ate up the short distance between him and his prey.

Then he kicked a nail.

Unwanted noise.

Terrell heard the chink of the metal as the nail skittered across the concrete. He spun around at the last second and—almost instinctively—his right hand balled up into a fist and traveled on a northwest path directly into the giant's lower jaw, slamming the behemoth's teeth shut. The blow sounded like a hardcover textbook being dropped onto a sleeping student's desk.

The Haitian was dazed and let the shank[1] fall to the floor.

Terrell immediately wrapped his mitts around his attacker's tree trunk of a neck and squeezed—right hand clamped onto the back of the neck, left locked onto the front, just under the chin. Fingers not even close to interlocking. But trying. Stretching. Straining. He formed a virtual vise-grip around the larger man's throat; the muscles in Terrell's forearms bulged. His forehead was pressed against the side of the Haitian's massive shoulder for leverage. From above, their perpendicular bodies formed a capital letter T. Terrifying.

After what seemed like an eternity, his would-be killer finally stopped struggling, and Terrell eased the man's unconscious, oxygen-starved frame to the floor. He didn't want to hurt the guy any more than he already had.

Pretty generous for someone who was just attacked by a monster.

For no reason.

Well, *maybe* there was a reason.

Pennsylvania Correctional Industries' shoe factory wasn't dubbed the *Sweat Shop* by the inmates for nothing. It was dirty, and it was *hot*. Walls-sweating, air-not-moving, can't-breathe *hot*.

Air conditioner? Not for the prisoners. That was only for staff. They're the ones who really needed it. Sitting on a soft chair in a small

---

[1] shank - homemade knife

plush office was hard work.

Cockroaches? Mice? Black mold? Common as a boat in Venice.

Why all the random buckets? For *Where the heck is this rainwater leaking from now?!*

Archaic machinery and rusty metal cabinets and lockers littered the U-shaped floorspace. Flickering caged fluorescent lights dotted the ceiling—well, to be totally truthful, the few lighting fixtures were suspended from exposed steel I-beams under a corrugated tin roof that *posed* as a ceiling.

Rotted wooden shelving was piled high with dusty boxes full of old product. Various skids of newly delivered raw materials were situated strategically around the perpetually filthy floor, waiting for their turn to be prepped and assembled into even more pairs of prison boots.

Twenty thousand square feet of *No I'm not having a good day!*

And the rest of the prison was just as decrepit.

Still, that's no excuse to *kill* somebody.

Terrell was puzzled. He paced back and forth along the length of the fallen giant. *I robbed this bouh[2] brother over two* years *ago. And I ain't even shoot him. I know he ain't put no hit out on me. We* been *squashed that. I gotta get on the horn ASAP.*

I ain't got no time for this; I'm tryin' to go home. *Glad it ain't no cameras back here... Let me go tell his homie to wake him up.* And that's what Terrell did.

Surprisingly, the Haitian's friend appreciated that Terrell had let him know what happened back there. No tag-team matches today. Besides, Terrell wasn't an easy mark. He was built like an elite NFL running back, and he moved with the grace of a panther.

As soon as he made it back to his work area and wiped the sweat from his face, his supervisor called him into the office.

The prisoner struggled to keep his composure. His mind was

---

[2] bouh - Native Philadelphia vernacular for the word *boy*. It's pronounced like the word *boar*, but without the 'r' sound

racing. *Man, I'm hit.*[3] But I don't know *how. Wasn't nobody else even back there. Ain't nobody see nothin', and main-man not no rat—he just tried to kill me. I knew I should've just went to the yard. Nineteen cent a hour ain't worth it.*

When Terrell entered the air-conditioned office, his supervisor said, "Jackson, you have to go back to your block and take the lock off your door. A bunch of new commits just came in."

"Alright, I'll be back." He left the office. *At least I ain't in trouble. I thought I was cooked!*

Relieved, but frustrated, Terrell Jackson took his time walking down the long corridor at SCI Graterford, one of Pennsylvania's most notorious prisons.

A new cellmate was the last thing he needed.

When Terrell made it to his housing unit, he spotted an inmate sitting at the table in front of his cell.

Terrell continued to stroll down the city-block-long tier, and under his breath he said, "This dude *better* not be no bum."

All that Terrell could focus on was his new cellie's unkempt, nappy-looking afro and shaggy beard. That usually signified a broke dude. If not for their light brown complexions and deep-set chestnut eyes, Jackson—tall with short wavy hair and close-cropped beard— looked the exact opposite of the newcomer.

Already resigned to the worst-case scenario, Terrell was thinking *I'ma have to feed him until he get a job somewhere. He better at least know how to cook.* Once he got closer, he mumbled, "Man, I *know* this ain't—"

The forever-chubby Malik Jackson got up from the table and yelled, "Yo, Bro'!"

Terrell broke out into a huge smile and, a moment later, embraced his biological brother. "'Lik'! I ain't know they was gonna ship you here! *And* we cellies?! This day keep getting' crazier! Yo, I heard you

---

[3] hit - caught

got booked and took a quick deal and was up Camp Hill."[4]

"Yeah, I got caught wit' a onion of hard.[5] When they offered me a four to eight, I *had* to jump on that."

"I ain't mad at you. You came *up*."[6] He glanced at the two brown boxes behind Malik, began removing the MasterLock from His sliding cell-door, and said, "Yo, come on and get unpacked."

"Alright. Hey yo, where was you at? I was sittin' at the table for like fifteen minutes."

"At work."

"You gotta go back?"

"I told 'em I was, but I'm cool. I gotta make sure my lil' bro' get dug in."[7]

"Solid. Well, wassup wit' you? You stayin' out the way? Or is you a hotboy?"

"Speakin' of hot, some bouh tried to light me *up* at work this morning."

"Real rap?"

"Real rap, Bro'. I work in the *Sweat Shop*—the shoe shop—in shipping and receiving. So, I'm in the back stacking some boxes, and Eric tried to air me ou—"

"*Eric?*"

"*Haitian* Eric. From 23rd and Tasker. 'Member I robbed his brother?"

"Yeah. *Yeah...* "

"Why you say it like that?"

"Naw, *I* had some words wit' his brother at *Chickie's & Pete's*[8] right 'fore I got booked. It ain't really go nowhere. We was both a little tipsy. He was just talkin' cute in front of his girl, but I don't play wit' everybody like that; that's all. He might've mentioned somethin'

---

[4] Camp Hill – State Correctional Institution at Camp Hill, PA

[5] onion of hard – 1 ounce of crack cocaine

[6] came up – made out well

[7] dug in - settled

[8] Chickie's & Pete's – a popular South Philadelphia sports bar

'bout it to Eric probably. But what happened, though?"

"Yeah, he tried to stab me, but I seen him at the last minute and dipped that jawn[9] and caught him on the chin. The banger[10] fell, and I choked him out, then I got out of there."

"Why you ain't down[11] him?"

"Bro', I be fallin' back now. I just told his man to go wake him up and that was it."

"You think he came at you over his brother?"

"I don't know. Me and his brother *been* squashed that."

"Naw, I'm talkin' 'bout *me* and his brother. What block he on? I wanna holla at him."

"'Lik, you just got here. You don't need to be gettin' into nothin'. We mess around and get out close to the same time, if we play it right. Just fall back. I got it."

"Naw, naw. I ain't 'bout no drama no more. I get money. You know that. I just wanna talk to him so don't nothin' else jump off."

"Oh, alright, that's cool. And I know we be stressin' Mom out, too. We gotta chill, Bro', for real."

"Yeah, you right. 'Specially on the drama tip. But I'm still tryin' to get this bread[12] when I get out though. I'm tired of seein' Mom struggle. I just wanna surprise her wit' her own house and a nice wheel..[13] She deserve it, 'Rell."

"Absolutely."

* * *

THE JACKSON BROTHERS were actually *half*-brothers. They had the same dad. Then one day, they didn't have a dad at all.

Mr. Jackson—a finely dressed man with an athletic build and

---

[9] jawn – extremely versatile noun, defined by context of conversation

[10] banger – homemade knife

[11] down - kill

[12] bread - money

[13] wheel - car

caramel-colored skin—had left Terrell with Malik's mother so that the two young boys could play together. He made sure that his sons saw each other at least three times per week. Mr. Jackson usually stayed with them, unless he had some other business to take care of. So, when the sharp-looking man told Malik's mother that he would be right back, nothing seemed out of the ordinary.

Until he failed to return.

And was never heard from again.

No one even knew if he was alive or dead.

Tragically, Terrell's young mother died two years later in a car accident. The orphan was one phone call away from foster care when Malik's mom stepped up to save the day.

But finding themselves without a positive father figure, the Jackson boys eventually gravitated toward the older hoodlums who hung out on the corner. And those young Jacksons were welcomed with open arms.

* * *

TERRELL CONTINUED, "SHE a gangsta for real. All I *got* is love and respect for her. I *still* be thinkin' 'bout what it would take for a female to adopt the son of the woman that her man cheated on her wit'. How real is *that?!* That's *major.*"

Perched on the metal desk and gazing out of the window of his new cell, Malik replied, "And that's why I gotta get major money. I don't want her to have to worry about nothin' else for the rest of her life. I already got somethin' nice put up for her out there. All I need is like eighty or ninety more, and she gonna be set. I wanna give her the spot[14] and the car all at the same time. The car gonna be sittin' right in her driveway."

"Bro', I'm wit' you, whateva you need. Just say the word."

Malik turned back to his cellmate and said, "I was dealin' wit' this Mexican bouh. We can get wit' him when we get out. Prices is right.

---

[14] spot - house

Product tight. Green[15] *and* white."[16]

"I know you ain't still rappin'."

"Gotta diversify my portfolio."

"Cut it out would ya? But yo, I'm definitely down to get this bread wit' you."

"My man."

"But right *now*, we gotta get you a haircut. I was grindin' you *up* when I was comin' down the tier."

"You know the Hill a rough stop. They burn you for everything—barbershop, yard, phones... Yo, I'm in the hut wit' 'Rell! J-B is in effect!"

"Yo, chill! You drawin'![17] Don't nobody know about the Jackson Brothers. You took it back to Stanton[18] on me. When we come up wit' that? Like the third grade? You still know the handshake?"

"*Do* I... "

---

[15] green - marijuana

[16] white – raw cocaine powder

[17] drawin' – drawing unwanted attention

[18] Stanton – Edwin M. Stanton Elementary School on 17th and Christian Streets in South Philadelphia

CHAPTER 1

*T*HE JACKSON BROTHERS had no idea that both of their lives would be hanging in the balance in mere minutes. But maybe they should have. In the streets, there are rules that should never be broken.

"Park right here, 'Lik," Terrell told his old cellie.

"*What?!* You tryin' to get me killed?"

"Man, I *always* park here. Stop trippin'."

"You *know* I don't play the block like that, *'specially* 17th and Annin! These youngbouhs is *wild* now. They downin' *everything*." Malik wanted to drive to a nicer neighborhood to wait on a customer. Because where *they* were—ghetto.

Two-story brick rowhomes with broken mini-blinds, trash bags or bed sheets covering the windows; a few long-abandoned vehicles in various states of disrepair; dirty sidewalks plagued with black splotches of old chewing gum; garbage-filled lots where houses once stood. And if a person cared to look closer—narcotics and firearms stashed all *over* the place. *Especially* in the lots.

From above, the 1700 block of Annin Street resembled a mouth with too many missing teeth. Ghetto

Terrell said, "You paranoid for nothin'. This *our* hood. Ain't nobody doin' nothin'.'"

"See? That's your problem. You can't *sleep* on nobody, 'Rell. You ain't the only one wit' a gun."

"It ain't about that. We put that work in[19] around here. They respect us, Bro'.'"

"You gotta give respect to get it. When we was gone, the block ran without us. They ain't need us. And we don't even *live* around here no more now. You keep comin' through bustin' traps like it ain't nothin' wrong wit' it. We ain't even puttin' these youngbouhs on no paper. All we doin' is makin' it hot[20] for em."

"Man, I used to have these dudes goin' to the store for me. You did, too."

"*Used* to. We been away for a couple years—you twice as long as me. They ain't our youngbouhs no more. They got hair on they face and egos as big as yours. I'm just sayin', this ain't back in the day no more. We don't need to make no enemies."

Terrell was quiet for a few moments, looking at the street behind him through the passenger-side mirror. Thinking.

* * *

1100 WEDNESDAY 25 NOVEMBER 2022: *SOUTH PHILLY*

"*Y*EAH, THEY IN the silver Accord parked in the middle of the block, next to the lot. Try your best not to bang 'em. This just business," said a deep voice on the other end of the phone.

"Well, they better act right. See you in a minute," Reds spoke into the Samsung Galaxy in his hand; then he turned to his partner and said, "It's on. Don't shoot 'less you got to, though. This just a business call."

Dressed in dark blue coveralls, the two armed-men exited their car and entered the alley on South 18th Street, between Ellsworth and

---

[19] put that work in – shot (at) people

[20] makin' it hot – drawing police attention

Annin. They quietly made their way past the rows of backyards, being careful not to alert anyone to their presence. The pair yanked down their ski masks right before they hit the lot.

And no, there was no need for them to pull the slides back on their pistols to chamber a round. This is the real world.

In the movies, people cock their guns when they think that they're about to get into something.

In the streets, a person will cock their gun only once. As soon as they get it; right after they load it. They *know* that they're going to get into something.

Sooner or later.

Always ready.

* * *

1104 WEDNESDAY 25 NOVEMBER 2022: *SOUTH PHILLY*
WITH HER LONG auburn hair parted down the middle and pulled into her signature pig-tails to show off her pretty Scandinavian face, Tara *knew* that she was drop-dead gorgeous. She was petite with a body known to stop traffic. The twenty-six-year-old beauty could have been a movie star. It's too bad that she liked getting high. She perpetually exercised bad judgement.

Tara had picked up an equally short, deep-voiced man earlier that morning, and they were now in the McDonald's parking lot at Broad and Carpenter streets. Waiting.

The man with the gymnast's physique went into her glove compartment and pulled out a black vinyl wallet which contained the vehicle owner's registration card. "Kevin *Hudak?*"

Her nerves already on edge, Tara responded, "Yeah. I *told* you that this is my boyfriend's c—"

"*I* know!"

"No, I was just saying because you read his name on the papers; that's *all*."

"Alright, whatever. I ain't worried 'bout dude."

"You don't need to be. Ma—"

"Hey yo, man, what's *this?!*" the deep-voiced man asked her while flashing a confederate flag decal that was adhered to the back of the wallet.

"What? His flag? That's for the *Dukes of Hazzard*. He's like a super-fan. He loves the south. That's where he was born. He's just a weirdo like that."

"Weirdo like what? What you mean?"

"He's just weird. I don't know."

"Yes you do. You said it. He weird like *what?* What you mean?"

"Like racist weird, I guess. M—"

"*Racist* weird?!"

"But you know that I'm not like that! That's why I said *he* was a weirdo! Not me! I went on my senior prom with a black guy! I *marched* with Black Lives Matter for George Floyd! And I'm with you all the time! You *know* me!" Tara had picked up on the sour expression on her illicit lover's face, but the damage was already done. She wanted to *kick* herself for opening her stupid mouth. Too much information. She knew that he wasn't going to leave it alone.

"What you mean *racist weird?!* You know who I am?! I'd *down* that—"

"No, no, it's not like that! I don't know! It's just that, one time we were watching *Planet of the Apes*, and he said something that caught me off guard. But he probably didn't mean it like th—"

"*What* he say?!"

"Okay, *okay*. He asked me, um, 'Doesn't this scene remind you of the ghetto?' I was speechless, and that was it. Kev—he never brought it up again." Tara lied. She looked out of the driver-side window feeling extremely uncomfortable. She didn't dare mention her boyfriend's other random racist remarks. *Why are we even* talking *about him? This is weird. Stupid sticker*.

After a rare moment of silence, the deep-voiced man said, "Look, I know *you* ain't like that, but don't make no excuses for dude, though. I *should* teach him a lesson since I got his info."

Tara attempted to talk him out of it, saying, "No, please don—"

"*Shut* up. That ain't got nothin' to do wit' you, but I know what *do*."

*   *   *

WITH THE FRONT-passenger seat leaning halfway back, Terrell broke his silence. "Hey 'Lik, I feel you, Bro'. I'm actin' like these dudes don't mean nothin' to me. I'm makin' they block hot, then I go back to City Line Ave like I'm better than them or somethin'. This where they live at. I *am* disrespectin' the block. This my last sale around here. *And* I'ma put Man-Man on." Terrell glanced at his phone and said, "Yo, what's takin' this chick so—"

Both of their doors flew open.

"*Do* what I tell you! Lift up that armrest—*slow!*" snarled Reds at a volume barely above a whisper.

Malik was beside himself. *How somebody get the drop on us?!* The younger Jackson already knew what it was. The cannon in his face was overkill.

Terrell looked like he was thinking the same thing. *How?!*

Malik didn't even dream about going for his pistol. The same couldn't be said for Terrell; *his* peacemaker was in the glove compartment.

Terrell could tell Silent Bob that the money was in there, and the elder Jackson might even be successful in getting to it; but his brother's cranium wouldn't stand a chance against a point-blank slug. Still, if he didn't try *something*, then the 'hood would think that they were sweet. And that would make them perpetual targets.

"My man, if you want the money, I gotta get it for you," Terrell told Silent Bob.

From the other side of the car, Reds replied, "Don't try to play hero. It's y'all brains."

Terrell glanced at Malik. And made up his mind. For better or worse, the elder brother sealed their fate.

Still shifting his weight forward, Terrell began to move his right arm backwards, but the formerly silent Bob blurted out, "What, you *reachin'?!*"

"Naw, naw, naw! The bread in my back pocket!" yelled a rattled Terrell.

Malik blurted out, "It is! It is! Y'all *got* it! The hammer[21] in the *glov*—"

"Shut up! Gimme the work!"[22] Reds shouted, cutting Malik off, then he glanced over at Terrell and screamed, "Get the money!" To B-O-B he said, "Get the gun!" Still barking orders, Reds told Terrell, "Pass the money this way!"

The muzzle of Reds' semi-auto never left Malik's head. *Intense.*

Their spoil now secured, the two masked bandits shut the car doors, backpedaled and sidestepped toward the lot with their guns still trained on the occupants of the Honda, and disappeared into the alley.

A Glock, nine stacks,[23] half pound of Cush,[24] and what look like six ounces of powder[25]—that ain't bad for sixty seconds of work, Reds thought. *My youngin' always do his homework.*

* * *

1108 WEDNESDAY 25 NOVEMBER 2022: *SOUTH PHILLY*

*D*RIVING AWAY, MALIK asked his brother, "Yo, you cool, Bro'?"

"No. I'm not! What was *that* about?! I ain't *never* see them before. *Nowhere.* They wasn't built like *nobody* I know. They ain't even *need* no mask."

"Yeah, they looked like stick figures. I don't know *who* that was. And why ain't girlie nev—"

"But what's crazy is, how they know about the *armrest*, though?

---

[21] hammer - gun

[22] work - drugs

[23] nine stacks – 9 thousand dollars

[24] Cush – a strain of marijuana

[25] powder – raw cocaine

I'ma ask around 'cause somethin' funny. It *had* to be somebody from the block that put 'em on us. Ain't no outsiders comin' through Annin Street—not like *that*. Not without permission."

* * *

*R*EDS AND B-O-B made it back to the 1800 block of Ellsworth Street and jumped into their getaway car. Reds made a left on 18th Street, drove two blocks, took a right on Carpenter, and pulled up next to the deep-voiced man and Tara at McDonald's two minutes later. Reds told B-O-B to stay in the car and climbed into the back seat of the Subaru.

The first words out of the mastermind's mouth were, "I ain't hear no shots."

Reds smiled and said, "Some dudes know how to get robbed."

The two men shook hands, and the deep-voiced man asked, "Did we come up?"

"Nine stacks, half pound of green, six onions, and a hammer. How we gonna break it down?"

"Y'all need the hammer?"

"Always."

"Alright. Gimme the work and a band[26], and y'all keep the rest. That's cool?"

"Let me get a little bit of this Cush."

"Go 'head. We good?"

"Four grand, some green, and a Glock, and it ain't even twelve o'clock? Absolutely."

"Bet. 'Preciate you, O.G.[27] Be safe. Tell B-O-B he my idol. I'ma catch up wit' y'all this weekend."

"Alright, be cool. 'Sup White Girl? Good lookin' *out*."

"What's up?" Tara said, nodding her head.

---

[26] band – 1 thousand dollars

[27] O.G. – a respectful term, short for *original gangster*, used to address an older hoodlum

Then Reds was gone.

The small man, in a noticeably better mood, told Tara, "Yo, I *bangs* wit' you,[28] Tee. You a rider.[29] I don't now *why* you wit' that clown. But I ain't gonna hate. You my lil' racist rider, that's all."

Tara said, "I *ain't* racist," and then she asked him, "Do you think that they're gonna know it was me?"

"Naw. You gonna go around there after you drop me off and act like nothin' happened. They should be gone when you get there, so call 'em and ask 'em where they at. Tell 'em you on the block. If they ask why you late, tell 'em you got pulled over speedin' on Grays Ferry Ave. They don't know you know *me*. They ain't gonna think no white girl they been dealin' wit' over a year set 'em up."

Tara pulled her rhinestone-encased phone out of her brown and tan leather designer bag to check a text message. It was Kevin—again. "Man-Man, I have to go. Where exactly do you want me to drop—What are you *doing?!* Give me my bag! Don't go in there!

Man-Man opened her matching wallet and said, "Now I got *your* info. If you *ever* think about sayin' somethin'—'bout this *or* your racist boyfriend—"

"You don't have to *be* like that! I ain't gonna rat you out! About *anything*, Man-Man."

"Hope not. Here go your cut."

And Tara drove out of the parking lot one thousand dollars richer. And "greener."

* * *

1120 WEDNESDAY 25 NOVEMBER 2022: *SOUTH PHILLY*
*A*FTER DROPPING MAN-MAN off a couple of blocks away from his house—due to the circumstances—Tara parked in the middle of 17th and Annin and called Terrell.

When he picked up, she said, "Where are you? I'm on Annin

---

[28] bangs wit' you – admire how one carries themself

[29] rider – one who is down to break the law (in this context)

Street."

"Somethin' came up. You still want that?"

"Yeah."

"Alright. Meet me on 52nd and Parkside in a half hour. You know how to get there, right?"

"Yeah, that's no problem." But it *was* a problem. *A half hour? Kevin's going to kill me.*

"Alright. Hit me up when you get there if you don't see my car," and with that, Terrell hung up the phone.

A worried Tara called Man-Man *immediately.*

Man-Man answered the phone, asking, "Everything cool?"

"No! I think he knows! I think that he's gonna *shoot* me! I don't—"

"Tee! Yo, *chill.* Tell me what happened."

"'Rell answers his phone all cool and calm, and just says that something came up. And he asked me if I still wanted that."

"And? What's the problem?"

"He told me to meet him on Parkside in like a half an hour. I *never* met him out there before!"

"Man, he *live* around there. All he gotta do is jump on the E-way[30] and he right there. He just got *hit*, Tee. Why would he still be on the block? He don't wanna be down South Philly right now. Ain't nothin' wrong. Just do what you do; don't be actin' all paranoid. And don't use that band I gave you, neither. Use the money you came wit'."

"Okay. *Thank* you, Man-Man. Are you *sure?*"

"Tee!"

"Okay, *okay.* Well, can I call you when I get there so you can be on the phone in case something happens?"

"Yeah man, hit me up when you get there. Just be cool. Everything *good*, alright?"

"'Kay. Bye."

---

[30] E-way – the portion of Interstate 76 that runs through Philadelphia; also called the Expressway

But everything *wasn't* good.

* * *

*W*HILE TARA WAS on the phone with Man-Man, the Jackson brothers were still together. Talking.

Terrell said, "That was Tara, the girl we was waitin' on. She said she on the block."

"That's what I'm tryin' to say. I think she had somethin' to do wit' it."

"'Lik, I *know* she had somethin' to do wit' it. I could hear it in her voice. You think I'm the only black dude she know?"

"Well, why don't she get no green off the other dudes, then?"

"She might *do*. I don't know. But I *know* she had somethin' to do wit' it. White people ain't never late."

"I know. So what you wanna do?"

"You know I don't touch no females, Bro'."

"Me neither. We ain't into *that*."

"Yeah, but I know she had somethin' to do wit' it. But I don't wanna put the pressure on her, then she run to the law. Wish I could hack her phone or somethin', see who she dealin' wit'."

"Yeah, *right?* But the streets gonna talk, though. Or somebody gonna do somethin' they don't usually do, or sell somethin' they don't usually sell. It's gonna get out some kinda way."

"Facts. Just be ready to move."

"Ain't no doubt. But what about Tara? We just gonna forget about her? I ain't sayin' do somethin' to her, but she gotta pay some kind of way. Since she wanna grab somethin' off you, just burn her. Take the bread and don't give her nothin'. Then look her in the eyes and tell her why and cut her off. We don't put no hands on her but she get the message, though."

"I'm wit' that, but I just don't wanna tip our hand too early, 'cause she could tell whoever she dealin' wit' that we on 'em. Let it die down first. The streets definitely gonna talk. Then once we find out whoever the dudes was and move on them, *then* we could check her."

"I like how you think. We just might be related."

* * *

O N THE SURFACE, the meeting with Tara proved uneventful. She spotted the familiar silver Honda sitting near a curb, said, "Hey Siri, call Seventeen," put her iPhone in the pocket of her door, and pulled in behind the Jackson brothers.

Terrell glanced up at his rearview mirror, grabbed something from underneath his seat, slipped it into his jacket pocket, and got out and went into the car of the girl who set him up.

"'Sup Next Top Model?" It killed him to be friendly with her, but the elder Jackson didn't want to tip her off.

"Hey 'Rell. Everything good?" Tara hoped that Terrell couldn't see her trembling. She was almost paralyzed with fear.

"Always."

Tara gave him the cash, he gave her the package, and the deal was done. Easy enough.

But underneath the surface was a different story. And for most people, what's underneath has a tendency to rise up.

Terrell was furious, snatching the end of that long red pigtail and wrapping it around his fist until his knuckles were pressed into that stupid white girl's skull.

How could you think I'm that dumb?! You just so happen to call me once everything over wit'?! And you think I ain't just see your hand shakin' tryin' to unzip your bag?! You think I'ma just let you go without makin' it right?! You like this gun in your face?! How 'bout I put it in your mouth and blow a hole through your cheek?! Think we could call it even then?!

Tara was terrified; a big black man grabbing her by the throat and clamping down until she passed out. She woke up—gagged and hogtied—in the trunk of the Honda that was going who knows where, while Malik followed them in the red sedan so that she couldn't draw attention to herself by kicking out a taillight or something.

Will he burn me with cigarettes, or pry off my fingernails, or scrape a cheese grater across my face until I tell him what he wants to know? What if he jabs a needle in my arm and gets me strung out on heroin and makes me a sex slave until I earn his money back? I can't! I'm dead! I am so stupid!

Fortunately, Terrell got out and closed the door to the red sedan just as a lone tear trickled down Tara's unblemished cheek—*before* any of that could actually happen.

Imaginations can be cruel sometimes.

When the elder Jackson got back behind the wheel, Malik queried him. "Did you ask her where she was all that time just to make sure?"

"Naw, 'cause she would've lied to me, and I would've been ready to do somethin' to her *right there*. And I would've *made* her tell me who did it so I could go at them."

"'Rell—"

"I know. That's why I ain't tip,[31] but I'm *hot* right now, 'Lik. It

---

[31] tip – fly off the handle

CHAPTER 2

*T*ERRELL SAW HIS brother's black Genesis GV80 parked in their mother's driveway. He couldn't help but to smile as he pulled up behind it. They both loved going there. It was the most peaceful place that they knew.

Terrell could already feel the stress leaving his body. Living a life of crime can take a toll on a person. He stepped out into the frigid air and walked up to the front door.

DING-DONG, DING-DONG!

"I'm coming," said a cheerful voice on the other side of the door. It was his mom. Youthful-looking and fit despite her fifty-two years. "Hey Babyboy!"

"Hi Mom," Terrell replied as he hugged her. "Where your car at?"

She answered, "*In* my garage with the automatic door."

And they burst into laughter. It was a running joke.

Their mom was extremely delighted with her new house and car, but the garage was the icing on the cake. She couldn't stop talking about it. "I got my own garage with an automatic door" was all that Terrell and Malik heard the day that they gave her the keys.

The brothers even filled up the house with new appliances and furniture and food—they expected a homecooked meal out of the deal—but that garage was something else. She could go from the kitchen to the car without ever stepping foot outside.

"Malik's on the patio. Go let him know you're here," she said.

Terrell smiled. "I *thought* I smelled barbecue. What part of Thanksgiving is *that*?"

"You know 'Lik. He's always doing something extra. He helped me cook all morning, but he said that he wanted to make something extra special for today. Go on back there 'Rell."

"I'm gone!"

Terrell slid open the door to the patio and said, "My man, why is you barbecuing on Thanksgiving?"

Malik replied to his brother, "My *man*, you should be asking me, '*What* am I cooking on Thanksgiving?' Lift up the lid."

"Yo! That's the turkey?! Look like that jawn got ran over," Terrell remarked. And he wasn't wrong. Viewed from above, it appeared symmetrical and flattened. An almost perfect square. Two wings in the top two corners. Two legs in the bottom corners.

"Bro', you ain't learn *nothin'* all that time you did. It's called *spatchcocked* or *butterflied*," Malik shot back.

"You should have your own cooking show: The Chubby Chef."

"Yeah, whatever. You just a hater."

"But naw, it *do* kinda look like a butterfly, though."

"Wait 'til you taste that jawn. Man, close the lid!"

"You probably the only weirdo in the world cooking out in the winter time," Terrell said as he complied with his younger brother's command.

"It ain't winter yet. And what you think people did 'fore they lived in houses? They cooked outside, genius."

"Well, since you know so much, tell me this: If the Koran really came from the Creator—"

"Here we go."

"Naw, check it. If the Creator wrote the Koran, then why you need another book to show you how to pray? How the Most High forget to put *that* in there?"

"Alright, you wanna do this? If Jesus is god, then why did *he* pray?"

"Do a female martyr get seventy virgins, too?"

"Let me ask you this: Do god lie?"

"No!"

"So we *both* agree on that, right?"

"Right."

"But Jesus lied. He said he'd be in the grave three days and nights, but Friday to Sunday ain't three days. So, since god don't lie, Jesus *can't* be god. He lied!"

"What, you rehearsed that?"

"Facts is facts, my man."

"For the record, they ain't crucify him on Friday, and he ain't get resurrected on Sunday. They killed him the day before a *high* sabbath, not the Saturday sabbath. It's in the Bible. He got crucified on Wednesday, and three days later is Saturday—*not* Sunday!"

"What, you read the *Bible* now? You gonna be a preacher?"

"Don't hate on me, my man. I got a gift."

"You got a drug habit."

Terrell laughed and said, "Naw, Bro', I read that in this book *They Lied.*[32] I don't know *how* I remembered that jawn."

"You read books, too? *Knew* that head wasn't big for nothin'."

Terrell jabbed his old cellie in the shoulder, and Malik yelled out, "Chill! I'm sore from working out, man!"

"What? Getting' out the bed and standin' up?"

I *told* you I joined *Planet Fitness*. I gotta get rid of this quarantine fifteen."

Bro'. That was a couple *years* ago. Everything *been* opened back up. And that look like twenty-*five*, not no fifteen. Don't blame Omicron for this right here," Terrell said while poking a finger into his brother's gut.

---

[32] They Lied – controversial nonfiction book about key teachings of Christianity by author Martseah Ehbed

"Man, whatever. I'ma be ripped *up* this summer."

"Is you finished? 'Cause it's bitin'[33] out here. I'm tryin' to go bust it up with[34] Mom. You talkin' crazy."

"Yeah, alright. But Jesus still not god."

"*Bro'—*"

"Alright, alright. I'm done."

The Jackson brothers went inside and found their mother sitting on the sofa in the living room. They sparked up a lighthearted conversation.

After the laughter died down, Ms. Bridgeford said, "Now listen, I know that y'all grown men and y'all gonna do what y'all want, but don't you think that it's time to try something different? Those streets don't love you.

"Guys get jealous, and they try to do something to you, or they get you put in jail. Y'all made enough money. Y'all *moved* me out the 'hood. Look, don't get greedy—and I'm not judging. But it's just that I know what kind of people you both are.

"Y'all got good hearts. Y'all could do so much for the old neighborhood. Everybody around there respect y'all.

"There's nothing wrong with getting a job and starting a business and showing the youngboys something better than what they're used to. You're grown men now, and men raise the village.

"You can do anything that you set your minds to. Don't limit yourselves. You're worth so much more than what you're *doing*. Just think about what I'm telling you, that's all." Ms. Bridgeford was hoping that they would listen to her.

* * *

2213 THURSDAY 24 NOVEMBER 2022: *OREGON AVENUE*
*T*HE JACKSON BROTHERS had left their mother's house a few

---

[33] bitin' – extremely cold

[34] bust it up with – talk to

hours ago. Malik dropped off his SUV and was now riding shotgun in the Honda with Terrell behind the wheel. Actually, Malik wasn't *riding* anywhere. They were both sitting in the Oregon Diner's parking lot, ready to tear into their slices of strawberry shortcake.

Terrell said, "Man, I was thinkin' 'bout what Mom said. We definitely made enough money. And she don't even know how right she was when she said, 'Those streets don't love you.' She worried about us. I *know* she wore out; *I'm* burned out, too. But I ain't lettin' that jawn go that easy. *Somebody* gotta pay. I ain't gonna just act like it never happened."

Malik let out a heavy sigh. "After sleepin' on it, man, we still here. I'm just ready to charge it to the game, Bro'. Let it go. Wasn't no shots fired. We get into somethin' and mess around and don't come out of it. 'Magine what that would do to *Mom*—both of us get bodied[35] or get life or somethin'."

"Yeah... "

"Man, we just gotta get out the game altogether. We already got the bread to do it. Plus we on parole. 'Nough is enough, 'Rell. We playin' wit fire. I ain't tryin' to get burnt no more. I'm ready to be *done* wit' it."

"What? Just knock off the rest of the work[36] and don't re-up no more?"

"Why *not*?"

"But not like *that*, though. First, we gotta find out who all got us. Make it right; so when we *do* get out, everybody gonna know it was on *our* terms, feel me? 'Cause if not, they gonna see it like we got robbed and got scared straight—straight out the game. Then every stick-up boy in the city gonna try us. It won't *never* end. Not unless we make a example out of whoever did it. Then we can walk away from the game wit' our head up."

"*Forget* the rep',[37] 'Rell! Ain't nothin' guaranteed! What if

---

[35] bodied - killed

[36] knock off the rest of the work – sell the remaining drugs

[37] rep' - reputation

somethin' happen to one of us?! Or *both* of us?! We right back in the joint[38]—that's *if* we ain't hit up[39] or dead. That would rip Mom heart out her chest, man. She *look* healthy, but her eyes is *tired*, 'Rell. We killin' her on the inside. For nothin'! We *set!* So what some little broke dudes stuck us up?! Look at all the dudes *you* jammed! Just charge it to the game, Bro'. It ain't worth it no more."

"I'm down to get out, but I gotta get out wit' respect. I ain't—"

"*Bro'!* Did you *hear* me?! Forget *us!* What about Mom?! All the crap we put her through over the years, man? Don't she deserve better than that?! She been through *enough!*" Malik was choking back his tears.

"Man... Look, I ain't you. I can't just change overnight. I'll try to leave it alone for Mom, but first dude come at us over this, I'm back in my bag.[40] I ain't gonna *keep* gettin' robbed."

"'Rell, they know we ain't soft, man. Ain't nobody gonna keep comin' at us. Ain't neither *one* of us goin' for that. I'm just sayin' we gotta chill out—no more offense, no more hustlin'. We *up* now, Bro'. We got the bread. We could let the connect[41] deal wit' Man-Man and just be done wit' it. It's a win-win. We put Annin Street on some *real* paper, *and* we out the game."

"*And* we could walk off parole." Terrell leaned forward and placed his left forearm across the top of the steering wheel, twisting his torso to the right. He looked at Malik and said, "I'm wit' that."

"Then that's the plan, then? No detective work?"

"No detective work. Knock off whatever else we got left and we done. You got my word."

"I know the change ain't gonna be easy, but it's gonna be worth it in the end."

"Yeah."

---

[38] joint - prison

[39] hit up - shot

[40] back in my bag – doing what one used to do; based on the context of situation or conversation

[41] connect – drug wholesaler

"So, what? I should call Juan and let him know we *done* done?"

"Yeah, go 'head. We *done*."

"Solid." Malik gave his brother a fist-bump, then he pulled a flip-phone from his inside jacket pocket, flicked it open with his thumb, punched in a single digit, and hit *Send.*

His supplier had given him the phone. A burner. The best kind—no GPS. One number saved in the contacts.

Yes, a flip-phone. Not the old kind, though. A 4G flip-phone with a touchscreen. But not cool-looking like the Z Flip. It was ugly; still had a physical keypad. The kind of phone that a young teenaged girl would lose on purpose. But it did the job.

A man with a heavy Spanish accent answered the phone. "Que paso mi amigo? You ready for me?"

"'Sup, Bro'. Naw. Me and 'Rell ain't gonna be grabbin'[42] off you no more, but we got somebody else to work wit' you. He good peoples. He 'bout that money."

"I don't understand what you say. You don't want my stuff no more? Why you change up *now*? You find somebody else?"

"Naw, naw. It ain't like that. We *done*. We gettin' out the game, but we got somebody who gonna take our place."

Terrell barged in. "What?! He *questionin'* you?! Put it on speaker!"

Malik complied, and Juan was heard saying, "— told you when we first make a deal this is long-term partners. You can't just quit, Homeboy. It don't work like that."

Terrell couldn't believe his ears. "I ain't no little kid you frontin' work to! We *pay* for what we move—up *front!* You don't *own* us, Dog! He said we out, so we out!"

Juan responded, "Maybe you not understand me. You don't quit. You finish when *we* say you finish. And you—"

"Who is *we*?! I ain't worr—"

"Sinaloa."[43]

---

[42] grabbin' - buying

[43] Sinaloa – the notorious, extremely ruthless Sinaloa drug cartel based out of Mexico

"My man, this Philly! We don't play them kind of games! You got guns, we got guns, too! If I say I'm out, then I'm out! Ain't no rap!"

"You not hard to find, Toughman!"

"Ain't nobody *hidin'!* I ain't playin' wit' y'all! You—"

"It's no *y'all*, Toughman! I don't need my soldier! I do this one myself!"

"Do what you gotta do!" Terrell snatched the phone from his brother and snapped it shut, disconnecting the call.

Malik looked at Terrell and said, "What was you thinkin'?!"

More serious than he had ever been in his life, Terrell replied, "I was thinkin' 'bout Mom."

"*How?* It sounded like you was thinkin' 'bout your ego."

"'Lik, ain't *nobody* forcin' me to keep puttin' myself out there. Not at all. Like *you* said, Mom deserve better than that. And maybe I do, too. We *both* do. We can't play the game forever; I ain't *stupid*. Sooner or later, everybody lose. Dead or in jail—I don't wanna be neither one. That jawn woke me up yesterday. I'm still sick[44] that we got robbed, but everything you said was true. Everything I said, too. I'm gettin' out, and I ain't lettin' *nobody* stop me. I ain't gonna go *lookin'* for no drama, but if it come our way, I'ma handle it."

"I feel you, Bro'. I ain't mad at you. And if it come, *we* gonna handle it."

"Ain't no doubt. Now go 'head and handle your cake. I see you keep glancin' at it."

"You right." Malik took a big bite of his cake, and with his mouth still full he said, "Yo, you wanna tell Mom tomorrow?"

"We could tell her right now; she still up. Probably binge-watchin' *Blue Bloods*. I'll call her since you got your hands and your face full."

After three rings, Elizabeth Bridgeford answered the phone. "Hey Babyboy! Everything alright?"

"Yeah Mom. Me and 'Lik got you on speaker. We got somethin' to tell you."

Malik started, "Actually, we was gonna surprise you tomorrow,

---

[44] sick – extremely upset

but—"

Terrell chimed in, "Yup. After tomorrow, ain't no more hustlin', no more robbin'—none of that."

"What?! I don't believe it! I've been praying for this day! I'm so happy for y'all!" trumpeted Elizabeth.

Malik said, "We serious, Mom. We *been* talkin' 'bout it, but earlier we made up our mind."

"Well, just about gettin' out the game, but you gave us—or at least *me*—some ideas about what I could do next," Terrell cut in.

"Yeah, me too, Mom. It's time to do somethin' positive. Not to mention that we still on parole," offered Malik.

Terrell said, "Can't forget that," and they all burst into laughter.

CHAPTER 3

*I*T WAS A chilly, overcast November day. But the Jackson brothers had no idea just how cold it was going to get.

Malik and Terrell had just served one of their customers and decided to get a quick bite to eat. They were in the McDonald's parking lot at Broad Street and Girard Avenue, finishing up two super-sized *Number 1s*. Milkshakes instead of sodas. Never mind the weather.

Terrell had to drop Malik off at a mosque at the intersection of 15th and Webster streets at 2 o'clock. No big rush. South Philly was only a couple of minutes away.

They sat in the car eating and talking.

"'Lik, this the last day for this madness. Tomorrow, we gonna be livin' in a whole 'nother world, my man," Terrell said.

"Can't be no crazier than this one. I'm *ready*. What's the first thing you gonna do?" Malik asked his brother.

"You sound like we 'bout to get out of jail or somethin'."

"That's what it *feel* like."

"Yeah, I guess you right. The connect is like the warden; you gotta get the green light from him 'fore you could do anything. The cops is like the COs;[45] they catch you doin' somethin' you ain't got no business doin', they book you. The customers is like your cellies; you gotta make sure you take care of 'em, make sure they got what they need, or they might try to steal from you or tell on you or do somethin' to you."

"*Bro'*. That could be like a song or poem or somethin'. You just broke that jawn down for real! That's heavy! You got that from somebody, didn't you?"

"Naw, that's just what came to my mind thinkin' 'bout it just now."

"Matter fact, I'm puttin' that jawn in a song. I'm stealin' that."

"Yeah, well, you know where to send the check. But it *do* kinda feel like we gettin' out of jail all over again. We 'bout to be free from all the drama, all the stress, *all* that. We could call tomorrow *Independence Day*."

"Yeah, the day we was free from the game. That's our new holiday. Yo, you alright sometimes."

"Yeah, well, don't think about huggin' it out. I still got my gun on me."

"You ain't the only one." Malik paused, then he said, "Yo, what we gonna do wit' the hammers? We should just throw 'em in the Schuylkill."[46]

"I don't know, Bro'. I ain't tryin' to be goin' around naked,[47] 'specially wit' bouh talkin' crazy."

"Ain't you the one who told Mom, 'No more shootin'?"

"*Bro'*. I said, 'No more *rob*—"

"'*Rell*, if we out, we *all* the way out. We could deal wit' the hypothetical if it pop up."

Terrell looked at his brother intently and sighed. "Alright, we

---

[45] C.O.s – prison Correctional Officers

[46] Schuylkill – the Schuylkill River

[47] naked – without a firearm

could toss 'em in the river after we make our last sale. I'm all the way done wit' it. And if Juan try to come at us, gettin' some more ain't about nothin' anyway."

"Facts. In the meantime, we could get some *real* jobs, not just on paper. Keep parole off our back for real."

"That's cool. Then we could branch off into our own business or nonprofit or somethin'. The 'hood *definitely* need help."

"And we *lived* it, so we know what kind of help they need, what kind of opportunities they don't get—everything."

"Yeah, we gonna put it together. That's what it's abo—"

PICK UP THE PHONE! PICK UP THE PHONE! PICK UP—

A startled Malik said, "*Stupid* ring tone. That's so 98ish."

"That's *money*," Terrell replied while looking at his screen. He slid the green phone icon upwards. "Wassup?... I *can* be... Yeah, I got that... Like twenty minutes... Alright."

Terrell turned to Malik, "Bro', we gotta make a pit stop, but you ain't gonna be late though. I got you."

"C'mon, man. It's already 1:20. Where you gotta go?"

"Bro', I *got* you."

"You ain't even gonna tell me, though?"

"You worry too much. Look at some TikTok videos or somethin'. Stop stressin' all the time. I got you," Terrell said as they pulled out of the parking lot.

Malik's brother drove like a maniac sometimes. And this was one of those times.

It seemed as if Terrell went from zero to sixty and back down to zero between every pair of stop signs. The crescendo of the V-6 could be heard from two tenths of a mile away; and then the sound of virtual silence as the elder Jackson came to a stop at each corner.

* * *

1323 FRIDAY 25 NOVEMBER 2022: *NORTHERN LIBERTIES*

*A*S RUSSELL PULLED up to the stop sign in his new-to-him four-door Toyota Tundra, a silver tinted-out sedan was speeding down the cross street, quickly closing in on the intersection.

Russell stuck his left arm out of the window and waved it on. "Must be in a rush," he said to himself. "*I* ain't mad at 'em. Just hope they don't get pulled over."

He also said a quick prayer asking for everything to be okay with whoever was in the car. Although food and shopping were on his mind—in that order—Russell's concern for people always took first place.

Oddly enough—aside from his milk chocolate complexion—he and Terrell Jackson could have passed for brothers. Same hair, same beard, same eyes, same build.

* * *

1323 FRIDAY 25 NOVEMBER 2022: *PARKSIDE AVENUE*

*W*HILE SLOWING DOWN the Honda, but still a good distance away from an upcoming intersection, Terrell saw a guy in an orange pickup truck motion for him to keep going. He said to his brother, "Bouh lettin' us go! That's wassup!" while stepping on the gas. "That's what we needed right there! But that hat *was* super bright, though."

"Who wear neon green *anything?* Bouh a weirdo," added Malik.

"Chill. Don't call him no names. He let us go through the stop sign. That's my man." Terrell sped on.

* * *

1338 FRIDAY 25 NOVEMBER 2022: *MIFFLIN STREET*

*W*HEN HE ARRIVED at his destination, Russell breathed a sigh of relief and said, "Finally home."

As he walked through the door, Russell's wife—decked out in pink pajamas and matching headscarf trying to hold back her 70s-era afro—asked, "You have a long drive, Babe?"

"When I'm away from you, *any* drive is a long drive."

"You know just what to say to keep me cooking for you. Come here. Tell me if you like this sauce."

"Kiss first. The sauce can—"

"Daddy!" A little wrecking ball of hair barreled into the back of Russell's legs.

"Hey, my little super hero," Russell said as he lifted his daughter into the air and spun her around. Giggles filled the kitchen.

Russell said, "Now that the gang's all here, let's pray and eat."

"Okay," his wife whispered.

"Okay," the little hero echoed.

Russell prayed, "Yahweh, for this meal, we give You thanks. In Your Son Yahshua's name we pray. HalleluYah."

Following her husband, Russell's wife said, "HalleluYah."

And one more little "HalleluYah" was heard before the feasting commenced.

CHAPTER 4

*H*AVING SHED HIS country grammar and southern accent for the most part; the Wheelwright, Kentucky transplant appeared to be a native Yankee. A Jersey boy to be exact. Black hair cut short and gelled down all around. Matching beard minus the hair products. Six feet tall, one hundred seventy-five pounds, and a smile to melt an iceberg.

But no one knew what was underneath the surface, except for his online brotherhood. And *maybe* his girlfriend.

Today was the day. Kevin—or KV as he is known in his virtual world—did the research, hashed out a solid plan, purchased the equipment, and secured the approval of his superior.

The online forum, *zookeeperz.net*, has nothing to do with animals and everything to do with hate.

Reeling from a tragic loss last year, KV stumbled upon the site by chance. It was destiny.

He thought that he was the only person on the planet who had a legitimate reason to hate the black race. It turns out that every one of the members of *zookeeperz.net* has allegedly suffered some kind of perceived loss at the hands of black people.

KV enjoyed the chatrooms the most. He really gained a sense of who everybody was. And bonds were formed.

He developed a friendship with a general in a bona fide, real-world hate group. They even spoke regularly on the phone. KV absorbed all of the info that he could.

The General, as he is called, knew that this was the big day for Philadelphia Sergeant—his moniker for KV.

The General was impressed with the level of understanding and sophistication that KV had acquired in such a short period of time, while KV was under his tutelage.

From deception to pipe bombs to homemade silencers to circumventing ATF regulations, KV had graduated into a full-fledged, homegrown terrorist. And today was the day that he would showcase his wicked skills.

Kevin was frustrated. He paced back and forth, wall to window, in his spacious bedroom and spoke out loud. "Where the heck is *Tara* at?! She's always getting high! Stupid woman! I could've confronted her a long time ago, but that might have spiraled out of control, and I don't need *any* kind of attention from the authorities.

"I don't even know why I keep her around. She's a liability. She could get into an accident—in my car—or get pulled over, or get kidnapped and gangraped by the monkeys that she buys her pot from, and then *they* would have my car. She thinks that I don't know. I'm not stupid.

"Where is she *at?!* Calm down. Be cool. You're the Iceman. You got time. You got *all day.*

"When this is over, you can get rid of her. But right now, you need her. A lonely white male receiving a lot of packages might raise some eyebrows, but a guy with an attractive, high-maintenance girlfriend wouldn't.

"Too bad that she loves *monkeys*—I *hate* that music. And what's funny about a man dressing up like a grandmother who carries a revolver in her pocketbook? Or is it *his* pocketbook? That's stupid. *Stupid* monkeys. I hate 'em...

"What was I saying? Oh, yeah. If Tara wasn't a monkey lover, then we could have been Bonnie and Clyde 2.0. Instead of robbing banks, we could've been exterminating pests and making the world a better place.

"Well, it'll definitely be better after today. She needs to hurry up. I have to go to my armory and suit up. I'm Batman. *I* am Zookeeper, defender of the civilized world; mild-mannered investor by day, and monkey slayer by night. Papa would be proud—"

"Who were you *talking* to? You're crazy," Tara told Kevin as she barged into the room.

"Yeah, you're *driving* me crazy," he fired back. "You were supposed to be here *hours* ago, and I still have to drive you home! It's going to take forever because they're working on the Grays Ferry bridge! Every time that I *give* you the car, you're hours late! What were you *doing?!*"

Turning on the charm, Tara said, "I was picking up some outfits that I *know* you want to see me in."

Her boyfriend *instantly* changed his tone, saying, "Look, Tar', just don't let the time get away from you like that, okay? And I'm sorry for throwing a fit. Come here." *A white bomber jacket and blue jeans never looked so good! I gotta snap out of it. But not right now.*

* * *

1342 FRIDAY 25 NOVEMBER 2022: *NORTHERN LIBERTIES*

*R*IGHT AFTER THE transaction was complete, Malik said, "Man, we ain't gonna make it. You *knew* I had to be there, 'Rell."

"Bro', I *got* you. I *had* to get that off. We almost out. One more call could do it," Terrell replied, easing out into the stream of vehicles and stomping down on the accelerator. He was using both lanes, weaving in and out of traffic.

Malik said, "Chill, 'Rell. Somebody gonna say you drivin' aggressive."

"We gotta hurry up and get there. I wanna get as close as I can 'fore I hit the little blocks.[48]

"Whatever, man. Do *you*. Just don't get us pulled over. I ain't tryin' to go back on no nutty jawn."[49]

That was all that Terrell needed to hear. He said, "Ain't no doubt," and hit the gas—buildings zipping by on either side.

Two close-calls later, and without one second to spare, Malik walked into the mosque. "This the last day for *this* crap," he said to himself as he kicked off his shoes.

Th game was almost over.

* * *

*R*USSELL TOLD HIS wife, "That was the best lunch I had today!"

"That was the *only* lunch you had today, Big-head," she replied with a smile.

"Exactly. You ain't got no competition."

"Shut up.

"No, that was good, Baby."

The little one chimed in, "Yeah, that good, Mommy-baby."

"Thank you, Princess," Mommy -baby replied.

"Now I can watch Veggie Tales? I done my nap," the little one asked.

Attempting to correct her grammatically incorrect daughter, Mommy-baby said, "I'm done *with* my nap."

"That's a good Mommy-baby. You watch, too," offered Princess.

Russell burst out laughing. He couldn't help himself, saying, "I'm sorry, Baby, but I should have been recording y'all! It would've went viral!"

His beautiful wife couldn't help but to smile. "Let's *all* watch *Veggie Tales*." *Now Russell, laugh at that*.

"Again? This must be my lucky day!" Russell exclaimed, trying to

---

[48] little blocks – small side streets

[49] nutty jawn – unnecessary arrest

impersonate a three-year-old. *Somebody help me!*

CHAPTER 5

*A*FTER A GOODBYE kiss, Tara got out of the car and headed down the worn concrete walk of a large modified Victorian row home. Kevin watched his girlfriend enter and shut the front door of her apartment building. He hadn't helped her with her bags. But only because she didn't ask. She knew that he had somewhere to go.

His red Subaru was parked next to the curb. Engine running. Heat pumping out of the vents. His foot on the brake. Hand on the gear selector. Eyes locked onto his reflection in the rearview mirror.

You're really doing this. I'm proud of you. No fear. No mercy. Let's go to work.

* * *

1459 FRIDAY 25 NOVEMBER 2022: *MIFFLIN STREET*

"*W*ELL, PRINCESS, IF you tell me what you learned on *Veggie Tales*, I'll bring you back a surprise from Walmart," Russell offered.

Princess answered, "Don't helpin' people hurt... can—don't helpin' people can hurt people!"

"If you don't help people who need it, you're really hurting them!

Good job! Keep an eye on Mommy-baby, and I'll be back in a little while, okay?"

"Okay, Daddy."

Russell turned to his wife. "See you soon, Sweetie. You need anything?"

"I did all my shopping online. I ain't crazy."

Russell couldn't help himself, saying, "Baby, you know it ain't good to lie."

"What?! I was on their website 3 o'clock this morning!"

"I know, but you said that you ain't *crazy*."

"Boy, bye."

"I ain't leavin' without a kiss."

"You ain't leavin' without a *fist?*"

"Oh, now *you* got jokes," he said as they embraced.

When Russell turned to leave, the little one blurted out, "Daddy, wait! We pray."

"Okay. Do you—"

"I do it, Daddy!"

"Alright. You ready?"

"Uh-huh," Princess nodded. She grabbed her daddy's hand and bowed her little head. "Dear Ya-wee, please let my daddy to be safe in the store and buy me lots too many surprises. In Yah-shoe name we pray. Ah-lu-Yah."

"HalleluYah!" Russell shouted.

With hesitation in her voice, his wife said, "HalleluYah." She turned to her husband and whispered, "Babe, please be careful. Princess never did this before."

He told her, "It's Black Friday. Ain't nobody thinkin' 'bout me. They thinkin' 'bout them Playstations."

"I'm serious, Russell."

"Alright. I'll drive carefully and pay attention to my surroundings. I will. And I got my ugly neon hat on. I'm easy to spot. I love you. And I love *you*, Princess!"

The little lady said, "Love you, Daddy! Bring back surprises to me!"

"I will!"

"Be careful!" his wife yelled as he walked out of the door. "And wear your mask!"

* * *

*T*ERRELL PULLED UP to the mosque at around 3 o'clock. His little brother hopped into the passenger seat and said, "Man-Man was in there, but he ain't really have no rap for me, though. He just greeted me and kept it pushin'. That was weird, right?"

Terrell lifted his foot off of the brake and replied, "Maybe he heard about what happened and ain't know what to say. That probably wasn't 'bout nothin'."

"Yeah." Malik gazed out of the passenger-side window and said, "Man, when you get jammed, it seem like *everybody* a suspect."

Making a left turn on Carpenter Street, Terrell blurted out, "*That's* what you was thinkin'?! Man-Man?! Bro', he day one.[50] He the *last* person—I couldn't even... But what if he got at Tara when I wasn't around? He *live* on Annin Street. He *always* there. She might've breezed through without callin' me, and he could've pulled her."

Terrell took another left—this time on Broad Street. No destination in mind. He was drawn to the congestion of Center City. The stop-and-go traffic helped him think.

Malik said, "What if you right? We still don't know who the other two bouhs was."

"But *he* do. I *know* he do. 'Lik, I see the whole jawn, now."

"No detective work, 'Rell."

"*You* the one that brung it up. It all add up. But you right. I'ma chalk that. And I'ma *still* give him a connect—not Juan, though. I don't know if Man-Man built for that."

"But if he really did it, and we put him on a connect, ain't that

---

[50] day one – a person that one grew up with

gonna seem shady to him, like we tryin' to set him up? He already actin' a little funny, like he think we know."

"Yeah, but we could just tell him that somebody got us, that it was a close-call, that it woke us up and we just wanna get out while we still can. And that's the *truth*."

"What if he *still* don't go for it?"

"Then we put him in the dirt."

Malik, totally speechless, just looked at his brother in amazement.

"We can't have *two* dudes on our head, 'Lik." Terrell stopped at a red light, glanced at the younger Jackson and said, "Bro', I'm *messin'* wit' you. If Man-Man ain't wit' it, then that's on him. I'll just—"

"Yo man, stop *playin'!* My emotions all *over* the place! I'm in the game, then I'm out the game, now you talkin' like we 'bout to be deep back in it! Right now ain't the time for *jokes!*"

"Let's go get you a vanilla Frosty so you could chill."

"You ain't even *listenin'*, man! Whatever." Ten seconds later, Malik said, "Hit the Wendy's on Delaware Ave."

"See that? I know *my* little Taliban brother—"

Malik punched Terrell in his shoulder—hard—then said, "Yo, stop *playin'* all the time, man. What was you sayin'?"

"Naw, I was sayin' if Man-Man ain't wit' it, that's on him. I'll just tell him to hit me up if he change his mind, but either way, I'm still gettin' out. So the space gonna be there if he want it."

"True. And it's gonna look good 'cause we ain't comin' at him on no meet-us-somewhere type jawn, na'am sayin'? Just passin' off numbers."

"Take it or leave it, 'cause we *definitely* leavin' it."

"Heard that. I ain't—"

PICK UP THE PHONE! PICK UP—

Terrell swiped up on the screen of his Samsung Galaxy and said, "Wassup?... All I got is a quarter jawn left... 'Bout to hit Delaware Ave once I get out this traffic; I'm downtown... Alright, bet."

Terrell disconnected the call, turned to Malik, and smiled.

His little brother asked him, "What you all geekin' for?... You a weirdo... Yo, man, *what?!*"

"'Lik, we 'bout to be out the game, Bro'! We 'bout to make our last sale! It's really goin' down!"

"You sure you ready to do this for real? I don't mean to bring it up, but we been down this road before. We was 'sposed to get out a while ago."

* * *

1402 WEDNESDAY 17 NOVEMBER 2021: *SPRINGFIELD, PA*

WHERE ARE Y'ALL taking me?" Elizabeth Bridgeford asked her two boys.

"Your favorite place. You said you was hungry, right?" Malik said to his mother.

"Oh, y'all didn't have to do this," she told him.

"Just wait," mumbled Terrell.

His mom asked, "What's that supposed to mean? Don't be having them people singing *Happy Birthday* to me. That's too embarrassing!"

"Mom, be cool. We gonna have a good time. That's all," Malik said to her.

When the trio pulled into Red Lobster's parking lot, Terrell teased his chubby brother, saying, "And don't eat up all the cheddar biscuits 'fore you get your food, Son. You gonna ruin your appetite."

"Man, shut up. You *lucky* I'm drivin'," snapped Malik.

I'll wait 'til you get out, Cheddar Bob," Terrell taunted, and then he smacked his little brother in the back of the head.

"Hey yo, man, stop *playin'!*" yelled Malik.

Elizabeth stepped in, saying, "Cut it out, Babyboy. He's trying to park."

If Malik would have been able to see his mother smiling, he would've lost it. Luckily for Terrell, she was looking out of the front passenger-side window, hiding it well.

Ms. Bridgeford loved her boys. Although she didn't give birth to

Terrell, she had a special place in her heart just for him.

That baby boy was only seven years old when his mother died. He didn't have any family left that she knew of. Except for Malik. Elizabeth wasn't about to let those boys be separated. Who knows where Terrell would have ended up? When it came to adoption, she didn't even give it a second thought.

No, she didn't like Terrell's mother while she was alive, but Elizabeth wouldn't wish death on anyone. She had a heart as big as a queen-sized bed. And her boys knew it, too.

While waiting for the meal to arrive, Malik asked his mom, "So, what do you think about movin' somewhere else one day? Like out the 'hood?"

She gave it some thought and said, "Well, I don't know. My house is paid for, and I already *know* everybody around there. Then, I would have to put my place up for sale, and probably still have to take out a small loan to pay the difference on the new house—*if* I can find one in an area worth moving to.

"Not to mention all of my furniture and appliances and knick-knacks. I'd have to hire movers. Then, if my house sells before I find a new one, I'd have to put all of my stuff in storage. It's just a lot to consider. I don't know. Why'd you ask?"

Malik replied, "I was just—"

HAPPY HAPPY BIRTHDAY TO YOU! HEY! HAPPY HAPPY BIRTHDAY TO YOU! HEY! YOU LOOK GODD! YOU LOOK FINE! HOPE YOU HAVE A GREAT TIME! HAPPY HAPPY BIRTHDAY TO YOU! HEY!

Elizabeth was facing the wrong way—her back to the kitchen—and the cake-carrying quintet of birthday servers got her good. She looked at them and said, "Thank you so much." And she meant it. If she was a server, that would be the hardest part of the job for her.

The boys didn't get off so easy.

"I told y'all not to *do* that! Now I'm the *Birthday Girl!* I'm never coming in here again!! I gotta find a new Red Lobster somewhere!" their mom growled, at a volume only loud enough for her boys to hear.

Terrell said, "Mom, we ain't mean to upset you or nothin'. We just wanted to do somethin' nice for your birthday. We thought that—"

"Boy, shut up. I ain't have that much fun all year! I got y'all! I really appreciate this. I'm glad I called off to— Hello! That was fast," Ms. Bridgeford said, now directing her words to the server delivering their food.

"You earned it ma'am. Here, I'll box up your cake for you," the young man offered.

"Thank you," she replied as he quickly carried out his task.

Terrell couldn't help himself. He had to mess with his brother, and so he said, "Cheddar Bob, they got your bis—"

"'Rell! You know I'm sensitive about that!" Malik shouted, and they all started laughing.

After the trio finished their late lunch, Malik told his mother, "This 'Rell treat. Let's go to the car."

You the only dude I know who don't never need no doggy-bag," joked Terrell.

Their mom asked them, "Do y'all ever stop?"

"No," the Jackson brothers replied in unison.

Malik pulled out of the parking lot, got into the left lane, and made a U-turn at the traffic light.

"Now where are y'all taking me? I don't need to go on a shopping spree," Elizabeth said.

Terrell answered, "Not too far. Malik just gotta take care of somethin'."

"Don't be selling no drugs with *me* in the car! I'm not going to jail!" exclaimed Elizabeth.

Malik said, "*Mom*, you watch too much TV. Ain't nobody sellin' no drugs. You trippin'."

"Well, how did you buy this jeep, then?" she asked.

Malik said, "You know what I'm talkin' 'bout. I don't never do nothin' wit' you around. Just be cool. We almost there."

After a few minutes, Malik pulled into the driveway of a house with a big red bow on the door.

"Don't they know that Christmas isn't 'til next month? And it looks like whoever you came to see isn't home anyway," Ms. Bridgeford commented.

"Yes she is. Come on. Get out the car, Mom," ordered Malik.

"For what? I don't know her," she said, still refusing.

"Yes you do. You better take a look in the mirror," Terrell told his mom.

"What are y'all talking a—bout?" As everything began to add up in her mind, Ms. Bridgeford's eyes welled up with tears.

"Come on, Mom, walk me to the door," said Malik.

While they traveled down the walkway—flanked on both sides by green, freshly manicured grass—Malik removed a pair of keys from his pocket and handed them to his mother.

"No you didn't. No you *didn't!* You bought me a *house?!* Is this my house?! Malik! Babyboy! What are y'all doing?! You bought me a *house?!*

Malik said, "The silver key open the front door. Go 'head, Mom."

Elizabeth unlocked the solid mahogany door, pushed it open, walked inside, and screamed. "No y'all didn't! No y'all *didn't!* What?! Thank you! Thank you! I can't believe it! I can't *believe* it!" She wrapped her arms around both of their necks and squeezed. Group hug.

The house—as far as she could see—was fully furnished. Their mom was in tears.

Terrell told her, "Nobody on this planet deserve it more than you. Come on, you gotta check it out, make sure you like it. We gonna give you a tour."

Even the kitchen was decked out. Samsung refrigerator, Kitchen-Aid stand mixer, Vitamix blender, All-Clad pots and pans, Le Creuset Dutch oven, LG induction range with a separate wall oven, quartz countertops—the boys went all out. Their mom was in shock.

Malik said, "Come on, we might as well check out the garage since we in the kitchen. You first, Mom."

Ms. Bridgeford walked through the door and said, "Shut up. You lying. No you didn't! A new car, too?! C'mon y'all!" Her voice couldn't go any higher.

Staring at her were the headlights and grill of a platinum Chevy Malibu. Terrell did the honors this time, handing his mom the key fob to her new car.

"I really don't know what to say. This is—I'll remember this day for the rest of my life," she said.

Malik told his mother, "At least sit in the driver seat to make sure it's comfortable and all that."

Ms. Bridgeford hit the button on the remote to unlock her doors. They all got in, and when she was adjusting her rearview mirror, she noticed a rectangular box clipped to the visor. She pulled it off and asked, "What's this for?"

Terrell responded, "It open up the garage door. Hit the white button."

When she pressed it, daylight began pouring into the garage as the door traveled up.

"I got my own garage with an automatic door! Look! I can drive right to work from inside of my house! I'm like a movie star ducking the paparazzi! I'm like Batman leaving the bat-cave! I don't ever have to step foot outside again! I can go from the kitchen to the car! This is too much!" exclaimed Elizabeth.

"We glad you like it. We just wanted to do somethin' extra nice for you 'cause you mean *everything* to us. Happy birthday," said Malik.

Terrell joined in, "Yeah, Mom, happy birthday."

"Get out of my car so I can hug y'all again," she said.

As the trio walked back into the house, Malik remembered something and said, "Oh, that's right. Use the gold key to lock the door to the kitchen 'fore you drive off on your missions. And that concludes your tour. Ready to go back to South Philly?"

"No," joked his mom. "I just want to sit in my new car, *in* my garage with the automatic door. I don't know what to do with myself. I feel like I'm leading a double life. Alright, let's go."

"Oh yeah, make sure you save this address in your phone GPS so you can make it back here. It's already programmed in your *new* car," mentioned Terrell.

"The one in my garage with the automatic door? That the car you talking about?"

As they all filed into Malik's SUV, he said, "Mom, you is *geekin'* over that garage door. That's all we should've bought you. We would've saved a whole *lot* of money."

Pulling out onto the street, Malik continued, "So, when you gonna officially move in? Once the deed come back, I'ma transfer it to you; the car title, too."

"Thank you, Sweetie-pie. And I'll probably move in next weekend. All I really need to bring with me are my dishes and utensils, my clothes, and my knick-knacks. The furniture and appliances can stay on Ellsworth Street...

"Now listen, I love y'all. And please don't take what I'm about to say the wrong way—I'm extremely grateful for today. But the only thing that would mean more to me than a new house and car is you two leaving the streets alone for good. That would be the best birthday present ever.

"Y'all could give the house and car back, move in with me, and get some jobs, and I'd be the happiest mom in the world," Ms. Bridgeford confessed.

Malik replied, "Me and 'Rell talked about that in Graterford, Mom. We workin' on it."

"Not the movin' in wit' you part, but the jobs. We *are* workin' on it. For real," Terrell quickly added.

"Look—and this is the last thing I'm gonna say—the thing with money is that you never think that you have enough. But that's a lie. As long as you have food and shelter, you'll survive. The rest is just decoration. Remember that," she concluded.

Terrell spoke up, "Mom, we don't plan on doin' this forever. Just lo—"

"Good," Ms. Bridgeford interrupted. "Now, let's talk about marriage and grandbabies. So, Malik—"

"That's for the old man! I ain't ready for that yet!" the younger Jackson said, trying to get out of it.

"'Rell is only three months older than you," Elizabeth responded.

"Yeah, he *old*. I ain't—"

"Boy, cut it out. Y'all *both* thirty-one. So—"

"Mom, *please!*" Terrell knew that it was only a matter of time before the focus shifted to himself.

Once the Jackson Brothers dropped off their mom, Malik said, "Man, she right. That was the plan anyway, 'Rell."

Terrell asked, "What you talkin' 'bout, Bro'?"

"Now that Mom set and we all the way up,[51] what happened to goin' legit?"

"I ain't ready yet. I mean, *you* all the way up, but I ain't have nothin' 'fore I fell. I wanna be sittin' on somethin' super nice when I get out the game. All I need is like three or four months, max."

"Well look, I ain't gonna leave you hangin'. Long as *you* in it, *I'm* in it. Just hope that we can make it out clean later on, na'am sayin'? That new D.A. ain't playin'. She be tryin' to roof *everybody*, 'specially hustlers. She don't be tryin' to hear *nothin'*. We gotta be on point. One more fall, we ain't getting' out 'til we old."

"Yeah, I feel you. We definitely gotta be careful. And I appreciate you ridin' wit' me, Bro'. For real. Four months, no matter *where* I'm at; and I'm already ahead of most. And I'ma fall back on them licks,[52] too. The burner strictly for defense, now. I don't wanna get you caught up in no nonsense you ain't have nothin' to do wit'."

---

[51] all the way up – financially wealthy or stable

[52] licks – armed robberies

CHAPTER 6

MALIK TURNED DOWN the radio and asked his brother one more time, "You *sure* you ready?"

"*Am* I?!" Terrell was all in. He couldn't wait to kiss the game goodbye.

* * *

1507 FRIDAY 25 NOVEMBER 2022: *GRAYS FERRY*

KEVIN WAS FULLY committed to the mission awaiting him. He pulled up to his storage unit, opened the lock, and went inside.

It was arranged like a miniature department store—a department store for Nazis. The posters on the wall were atrocious. They depicted crime scene photos of deceased African Americans in various states of decay. In one corner stood a suit of armor with the initials *WK* etched into the breastplate.

In another corner was a floor safe containing nearly eighty thousand dollars, three fake passports, a small address book, and a watch. A Hublot Big Bang. All black, ceramic bezel, silicone strap. He put that on.

Pipe-bomb components filled a plastic chest of drawers. Cases of .223 ammo were piled almost to the ceiling. Two unused gas masks—with canisters—sat on opposing sides of a small desk. A loaded .40 caliber EAA Tangfolio handgun on a third side. Eight neatly stacked 30-round magazines filled with some of that .223 ammo on the fourth side—the only thing missing was an assault rifle to fire it.

But that would be taken care of later on.

In a large rectangular plastic bin, there were different colored sets of army-style fatigues known as BDUs—Battle Dress Uniforms. Everything from desert camo to solid black.

Kevin went with the Mossy Oak pattern—he *was* going hunting today. He had a sick sense of humor. With his uniform selected—matching cap on his head, black Hi-Tek boots on his feet—it was now time to gear up.

Hudak donned his nylon web belt, adorned it with pouches, and filled the pouches with military-grade tear gas canisters, a scalpel-sharp KA-BAR knife, a pair of tethered silicone earplugs, a Surefire tactical flashlight, and a stun gun.

He took the pistol from the desk, slipped it into a neoprene Uncle Mike's holster, and tucked it into his waistband.

Kevin dropped a homemade steel-wool-stuffed silencer into the right cargo pocket of his pants. Into his left cargo pocket, he placed two of the 30-round mags—opposing ends taped together for rapid reloading. He dropped another pair of mags into his front right pants pocket. A pair of 6-mil nitrile gloves made their way into his back left pocket.

Before putting on the camo jacket, he strapped on a low-profile Kevlar vest. Just in case. The General taught him to always go the extra mile when it came to personal safety. The jacket was a bit oversized by design. Kevin didn't want his fully-stocked midsection—or torso—to betray him.

He grabbed the last two pairs of mags and dropped one into each of the jacket's waist pockets.

The final and most critical piece of equipment—a wallet containing his Pennsylvania driver's license and $1,000 in cash—

wound up in a chest pocket.

And who could go anywhere without their smartphone? Front left pants pocket.

Ready for war, Philadelphia Sergeant exited his 10 x 10 foot armory and got into his car. If all went according to plan, he would be back to prepare for round two.

He didn't turn on the radio for *this* trip. He could party later on. Right now, it was time for business.

He was in his element. He was made for this. He drove toward his destination with a cold determined look in his eye.

Then a police cruiser got behind him.

Everywhere that he turned, the patrol car turned as well. *Why are they still following me?! Don't they know that I'm on their side. I'm one of the good ole' boys...*

Did somebody tip them off? No one knows about today, except... The General. But he wouldn't rat me out. He's too involved. But what if he was a federal agent and he sent the police to catch me red-handed? But wouldn't he make the collar himself? This is a Homeland Security issue. They wouldn't ask the Philly cops for assistance...

What if the self-storage unit has hidden cameras? If I get pulled over, I'm not—

WHOOP-WHOOP!

The patrol car blipped the siren and flashed its lights.

Kevin was a nervous wreck as he pulled his Subaru into an Asian market's parking lot. But he wasn't too nervous to draw his handgun and tuck it underneath his thigh. Just in case.

"Nothing's going to get in my way today," he said under his breath.

The two patrolmen exited their car, took *maybe* two steps toward the red Subaru, and froze in their tracks. The officers looked at each other, lunged back into their vehicle, and sped off with the siren blaring, their red and blues lit up.

"Yeah! This is my destiny! *Tuh-hee!* I can't fail!" an ecstatic Kevin shouted behind closed windows.

The police car raced away to respond to a call of a man with a gun.

If only those cops knew.

The traffic wasn't too bad, considering what day it was.

Have to watch out for bad drivers. The last thing I need is an accident... I need to stop thinking so negatively all the time. Or am I just cautious? I know that I'm not paranoid; I'm the coolest guy I—

BUZZ-BUZZ-BUZZ, BUZZ-BUZZ-BUZZ.

Kevin's phone was vibrating. Irritated, he sighed, "What now? Who is—Oops!"

His phone slipped out of his hand and fell down by the side of his seat. He glanced down real quick to see if he could spot it.

With his eyes on the road, he slowly reached between his seat and the door. He didn't feel a thing.

"Where the heck is it?!" he asked out loud.

Then he took another look. A two-second-long look. He never saw the red light.

SCREECH!

Kevin's fingers barely managed to grasp the phone as his head snapped up at the unmistakable sound of a vehicle sliding to a stop.

He saw the side profile of an ugly orange pickup truck in his rearview mirror as he motored on.

He looked at the missed call and said, "Why is Tara calling me, *anyway?* I just dropped her off. I'll talk to her later. I have to *focus.*"

* * *

"*D*EVIL, IF YOU only knew what I was gonna be *after* the storm, you wouldn't have bothered me!" Russell couldn't help but to dance in his seat. He was in his truck singing along to one of his favorite songs.

"Yeah! But now I'm stronger! Uh! And I got more power! Uh-huh!

"And I'm a little bit wiser! Yeah! And I got more strength! Hey!

"I got—"

Russell slammed on his brakes. "Yo! That car just ran the light! Let me turn this radio down, man. Sorry Tye,[53] but I gotta be on point. We can finish our duet later."

Russell was talking out loud. That red sedan had startled him. He pulled over at a Wawa for a few moments to regroup.

* * *

1524 FRIDAY 25 NOVEMBER 2022: *DELAWARE AVENUE*

*A*T A RED light, Malik turned down the radio again and said, "Yo, I know I keep on asking you, but this about to be it, though. You good for real?"

"Man, I feel like I'm on top of the *world*. I ain't gonna let *nothin'* stop me now! Too legit to quit, Bro'! I'm good! I'm wit' it!"

"Hammers, too?"

"You already know! And your Zebra under your seat, too."

Zebra. Not the animal. A gun. Kel-Tec. Not black and white like the equine. Black and gray, like urban camouflage. Combat-ready. No safety. Ten rounds in the clip. One in the chamber. Heavy trigger pull. No accidents. Twelve pounds of pressure is what it takes to get the party started.

Malik slipped the compact nine-millimeter pistol into the pocket of his red vest, sunk back into his seat and exhaled—relieved and happy. They were finally doing it.

After cruising on Delaware Avenue for a few minutes, Terrell got into the left lane and began to slow down, preparing for a turn.

Malik asked him, "What happened to Wendy's? Where we goin'?"

"Walmart."

"On Black Friday? You *trippin'*."

"Naw, that's where bouh want me to meet him at. Plus, the parkin' lot gonna be crowded. That's the best time."

---

[53] Tye – Tye Tribbett, a gospel recording artist

"True."

* * *

*H*AVING FINALLY MADE it to Walmart, Kevin drove up to the entrance, paused to let some shoppers use the crosswalk, and took a look inside. He liked what he saw.

Hudak smiled all the way to his parking space. He had to park near the back of the lot, but it didn't matter. He made it.

Gazing into his rearview mirror—into his own eyes—Philadelphia Sergeant said, "This day couldn't be more perfect! Wall to wall monkeys! I got myself a shootin' gallery! I'm the Lone Ranger. I'm a White Knight. I'm the White-power Ranger.

"*Tuh-hee! I* am Zookeeper. I'm the Punisher. I'm an Avenger—Philadelphia Sergeant reporting for duty, sir. *Tuh-hee!*

"I'm the man. I'm ice cold. I'll put 'em all on ice. This is *my* day. *I* call the shots. Today is the day...

"Mama, they won't get away with this. They think that they didn't do nothin' wrong. I'll teach 'em. Pain is the only thing monkeys understand. Ain't that right, Papa? They're actin' up, and I'm gonna fix 'em good. For Mama.

"Fat, black, stinkin' monkeys. You killed my mama, and now I'm gonna kill *you*. Hey, you fat black apes and you old lady orangutans, the Zookeeper is here. You're all gonna pay for what you did last year."

CHAPTER 7

I CLOSED THE office up early for this?! I guess they're not worried about Covid anymore, Mrs. Hudak said to herself.

Walmart's parking lot looked like Times Square on New Year's Eve, occasional facemask notwithstanding.

"Mom, just stick close to me, and you'll be safe. These monkeys can get aggressive," her son distastefully remarked.

"Kevin! I will not tolerate that kind of language! I raised you better than that!"

"Yeah, when you had the time."

"I had to provide for us! We didn't have Tyler anymore! I had to learn a *lot!* Why do you always blame me for everything?! I did the best that I could! You said that this would be a fun shopping trip, and we're fighting before we even make it *into* stupid Walmart!"

"I don't want to fight, Mama. I'm just being true to my feelings. You have a right to disagree, just like I have a right to call people monk—"

"Kevin. Hudak. *Enough!*"

"Amendment number one of the United States' Constitution

states that—"

"Why do I even bother?!" Mrs. Hudak sighed. You're a grown man, now. You're successful. You need to find a wife and go out on your own. Why are you *torturing* me?!"

"I'm sorry, Mama. I *do* want you to have a good time today. What's the name of the oven that you wanted to look at?"

Once inside, Kevin and his mother had to wade through masses of people. Social distancing went out the window a long time ago. It was a circus—children screaming, couples arguing, people shoving each other. Black Friday at its finest. And Kevin's childhood was no different...

* * *

2001: *WHEELWRIGHT, KENTUCKY*

*N*O CHILD SHOULD ever be forced to watch their mother get beat up. Especially on a schedule that a person could set their watch by. Fortunately for little Kevin Hudak, it was his neighbor's mother.

But *Mr.* Hudak was the one doing the beating.

"No! Please! PLEASE! Why are you do—" Mrs. Bradshaw never got the chance to finish her sentence.

With a sharp crack reminiscent of a .22 rifle, Mr. Hudak's fist slammed into the orbital bone of his widowed African American neighbor. And the small lady went down *hard*.

"See, boy? This is whatcha do ta monkeys! When they get ta actin' up, ya put 'em in they place! Pain's the only thing they understand." Tyler Hudak's breath reeked of cheap whiskey and cheaper cigars. And so did his dirty white tank top.

The cowardly father ushered his son onto their own porch.

"She ain't movin' no more, Papa," seven-year-old Kevin remarked.

Mr. Hudak, not realizing what actually happened, replied, "Serve her right. I tell that monkey ever' week 'bout dat dang porchlight. Told her not to have it on when I—"

BOOM!

Little Kevin's ears were ringing something awful. And his daddy was missing part of his head.

Marcus Bradshaw was peeping through the blinds. He wanted to turn away from the beating that his mom was getting, but he couldn't. He felt as though, if he didn't watch, then he would be betraying his mother in some way.

Even through the closed kitchen window, Marcus heard the punch connect and saw that his only surviving parent was no longer moving.

When Marcus observed his neighbor from hell walking away like nothing even happened, something inside of him snapped.

The ten-year-old boy raced into his mother's bedroom and snatched his daddy's shotgun from the top of the closet.

It was always loaded.

Marcus' mom often told her son that if the white man from next door ever tried to come into her house, that she would blow his brains clear over the pecan tree.

With only socks to protect his fast-moving feet, Marcus disengaged the safety just as he made it out of the front door.

He could hear his father's words replaying in his head. "Ya might not have time ta cock it. Only thing ta do is take off the safety and pull the trigger."

While Mr. Hudak was in mid-sentence, that's just what little Marcus did.

He crept up behind that side-facing porch swing, raised up the barrel of that 12-gauge until it was about two feet away from the back of his evil neighbor's head and—*BOOM!*

Marcus' hands were stinging, and his shoulder was throbbing. He dropped the shotgun, raced over to his mother, fell down on her lifeless body, squeezed his eyes shut, and trembled violently.

Kevin was all alone with his father's corpse. "Papa! Papa! Get up! You're bleedin'! Your head broke! We gotta fix your head, Papa!

C'mon, get up!" he pleaded.

Shock set in quickly.

Little Kevin ran to the road shouting, "Papa bleedin'! Papa head broke!" over and over until exhaustion got the best of him, and he sat on the ground.

Thankfully, Mrs. Hudak was driving down her street just ten minutes later.

To her horror, she saw her little boy sitting Indian-style by the side of the road, rocking back and forth, pressing down on his knees.

The deeply-tanned brunette slammed on the brakes, dashed around the front of the pickup, scooped up her young son into her arms, and asked, "What's the matter?! What happened?! Where's Papa?! Kevin! Can you hear me?!"

She ran down the walk toward her house yelling for her husband. "Tyler! Tyler! Ty—"

Mrs. Hudak saw a slumped-over figure to her right. "No. No! TYLER! Somebody help! Some—"

And that's when Jessica Hudak noticed the Bradshaws lying in the dirt between their houses. She didn't know that little Marcus was still alive.

"Oh no. Oh no. Kevin, what did you do? Not the neighbors. Not your da—"

HONK! HONK! HONK!

Someone was leaning on their vehicle's horn. Mrs. Hudak was blocking the road. And that sound brought her back to reality.

Waving frantically, Jessica shouted, "Hey! Help me!"

The off-duty sheriff's deputy stepped out of his black Ford Expedition, hurried down the walk, and asked the distraught woman, "What's the problem, Ma'am? Is someone hurt? Oh—*my*. Don't. Touch. *Anything*."

Beaver Road was the talk of the town for months. Thankfully, little Marcus Bradshaw was allowed to move in with his grandparents during the investigation. He was never charged with a crime, but was given mandatory psychiatric counseling until his eighteenth birthday.

Finally cleared of any wrongdoing, Mrs. Hudak—just twenty-four years old and already a widow—deposited her check from the life insurance company, loaded up her late husband's white Ford Crown Victoria, and took her little boy all the way to Philadelphia, Pennsylvania.

The media circus had taken a toll on the surviving Hudaks. It was time for a change.

* * *

2001: *PHILADELPHIA, PA*

*T*HE WIDOW AND her young son landed in South Philadelphia, 10th and Jackson Streets to be exact.

Surprisingly, the racial climate in their new neighborhood wasn't much better; only more discrete. The area—concrete sidewalks and brick rowhomes as far as the eye could see—was predominantly white, and on the surface, there didn't appear to be any problems. That was Jessica's reality.

For little Kevin, he might as well have lived in a different zip code. The kids that he befriended and hung out with were brutal. They would chase any black children—especially boys—who passed through their turf.

If the "intruders" were unlucky enough to get caught, then they would get beat, and beat *badly*. Hockey sticks, baseball bats, broomsticks, fists and feet—the violence was breathtaking. In a bad way.

Years of witnessing and participating in this type of barbarism only served to further damage Kevin's psyche.

Jessica Hudak's only child had become a dangerous young man. All he needed was an excuse.

CHAPTER 8

"OKAY KEVIN, I'M sold. Walk me to the ladies' room, and then I'll let the clerk know that I want to buy it," Jessica told her son.

"Good. I think that's the best one. I can't wait for you to bake your famous peanut butter pie in it."

"That'll be the first thing I make for you."

The shopping trip was turning out to be a fun day after all.

As mother and son were making their way to the restrooms, the P.A. system blared, "Attention Walmart shoppers, the last of our Sony Playstations are being put out for purchase now. It's first come, first served. Once the shelves are empty, we will have no more in stock until December 6th. Thank you for—"

The race was on.

Well, it was more like a stampede. People were running and hollering and pushing each other, trying to get to the Electronics department as fast as they could.

And the Hudak's were right in the middle of the oncoming traffic.

Jessica had never seen anything like this in her life. She saw a young boy, no more than eleven years old, fall to the floor and get trampled on.

Someone with a shopping cart was steamrolling their way through the crowd and had knocked Jessica off balance. Kevin tried to grab his mother's arm to steady her, but a 270-pounder plowed right through the middle of them, sending Kevin crashing onto the linoleum floor tiles.

Mrs. Hudak managed to grab onto the edge of a shelf to regain her footing. But watching her son struggle to get up was more than she could bear. "Kevin—"

That was all that Jessica was able to say before a sharp pain took her breath away and caused her to fall to the floor clutching her chest. The blows to her head from the shoes of the shoppers as they ran past didn't help the situation any.

The still-young Mrs. Hudak suffered a major heart attack and failed to make it out of Walmart alive. Only three weeks away from her forty-fifth birthday.

CHAPTER 9

*P*HILADELPHIA SERGEANT PUT his .40 caliber pistol back into the holster and exited his car. Hopefully, not for the last time. He activated the alarm and marched off to war.

A maniac on a mission.

He struggled to maintain his composure as he entered Walmart. He was beside himself with excitement. He was really doing it. He felt like a one-man army—a trained soldier.

An entire year of studying and planning and target practice and waiting. Today was the culmination of fifty-two weeks of mourning and a lifetime of hatred.

"Good afternoon. Welcome to Walmart," the dark-skinned greeter said with a smile.

Philadelphia Sergeant simply smiled back. *Clueless monkey. I wish that I could've brought more ammo, but there wasn't enough room. Two hundred forty rounds will have to do.*

There were *Black Friday Sale* placards posted every fifteen feet—a cruel reminder as Philadelphia Sergeant waded through the sea of predominantly African American shoppers on his way to the Sporting Goods department. *Mama, we might not have come from money, but you definitely did the right thing with Papa's life insurance. Stupid monkeys would have blown it. They don't know* what *to do with money. We buy stocks and they buy cars. Idiots.*

* * *

*T*HE SILVER ACCORD parked in front of Home Depot.

Terrell called his customer and asked him where he was and then blurted out, "You *in* there?!... Alright. Gimme like five minutes. I'ma park a little closer. Me and 'Lik gonna meet you in the bathroom... No cameras... Always."

Malik looked at Terrell and said, "*Bro'*, I know you feelin' good and all, but you talkin' 'bout goin' *in* Walmart to make a sale. *In* there. Wit' major work on you. You ain't thinkin' straight. Why don't he just meet you out here? Let him buy what he buyin' and come to the car."

"I don't know how long that's gonna take; it's Black *Friday* lines in there. I'm just tryin' to get rid of this jawn and be done wit' it."

"And *why* I gotta go wit' you?"

"'Cause you got the gun."

"Your jawn in here, too."

"'Lik, this our last drop-off. Just make sure everything go smooth."

"Man, we goin' to jail."

"You worry too much."

"You don't worry *enough*."

"You—Here we go right here," Terrell said as he pulled into a good parking spot just vacated by a white SUV. "See that? Everything working out already. We out."

* * *

*R*USSELL ARRIVED SAFELY at Walmart. He had to park a mile away from the entrance, right next to a red Subaru Legacy. He got out of his truck and heard clicking coming from under the hood of the

Subaru. Exhaust headers cooling down. Metal contracting.

"Probably the same car that tried to kill me. They must've just got here, too. Black Friday make people go *crazy*," he mumbled as he folded in his side-mirrors and set the alarm on his burnt-orange pickup truck.

Russell had wanted one ever since he was in prison. Four years later, he was living the dream—*his* dream. Wife, kid, house, ministry, truck. He adored that truck. The inside was co clean that you could eat off of the seats.

Russell walked through the double sliding-doors and braced himself. *Man, this jawn is packed. I gotta get out of here 'fore the Sabbath[54] start.*

Even this early in the day, it was a madhouse. As soon as the clerks delivered items to the shelves, they were snatched up. It actually got so bad that customers were grabbing goods directly off of the pallets as they were being transported by the employees.

Gotta love South Philly people. Like I ain't one of 'em. But most people don't know 'less I tell 'em. I like that, though. It's hard to figure me out. Can't put me in no box—

Okay! Electronics! And they still got the memory cards! Let me grab these first, 'fore I geek out over the tablets.

---

[54] Sabbath – Biblical day of rest and worship, observed from sunset Friday to sunset Saturday

CHAPTER 10

SO MUCH NOISE. I don't see why they let these monkeys play that music that loud. Next thing you know, they'll be trying out barbecue grills, thought Philadelphia Sergeant.

Out loud, he said, "Okay, here we are," walking up to the gun counter.

Philadelphia Sergeant wasn't a gun nut in the classic sense of the phrase, because *collecting* firearms could get him placed on law enforcement's radar.

Rule Number One: Never draw attention.

Once he was known, he couldn't become unknown.

But renting firearms at gun ranges and lusting over them and researching them on the internet was harmless. And so was buying ghost guns. But Sleepy Joe was trying to change that. Little more risky now.

"Hi. If you need any help, just let me know," the middle-aged sales associate told him.

Philadelphia Sergeant replied, "Will do. Thanks." *Now that's a skinny white guy. Rifle probably weigh more than him. Especially that 3-0-8. Alright Kevin, enough. Quit daydreaming. You have a job to do.*

There were so many beautiful instruments of death. But he wasn't there to fantasize about steel and exotic woods and metal alloys and supple rubber and high-tech plastics and feet per second and foot-pounds. He was there for an AR-15. A seven hundred ninety-nine dollar *Bushmaster* AR-15. All black. Built-in flash-suppressor. Low recoil. Highly accurate. Extra loud. Fear factor times ten.

He'd been shooting the same one at a gun range for the past year.

"Excuse me, Michael," Philadelphia Sergeant said, reading the employee's name tag. "I think I know what I want."

Michael replied, "Great! And what will you be purchasing today?"

"The Bushmaster AR-15—the one on sale."

Taking the customer's outfit into account, Michael asked him, "They allow you to hunt with those things?"

"Absolutely. The more accurate, the better. Less chance of a bad shot and the animal suffering needlessly."

"How long have you been hunting?"

"Oh, since I was about seven or eight."

"Here we are," Michael said after removing the yellow security cable from the trigger guard of Mr. Hudak's new assault rifle.

While Philadelphia Sergeant was looking it over and peering through the sights, Michael asked, "Do you need a scope? We have so—"

"Got one. Custom made. Beautiful optics. Solid as a rock. A good scope is just as—if not more—important than the gun. Once you find one that can read your mind, you stick with it." Philadelphia Sergeant lied. He had never even used a scope.

Rule Number Two: Make fiction sound like fact.

Michael replied, "I see. Well, we'll have to do a little paperwork. Shouldn't take too long. And I'll need to see some ID."

Philadelphia Sergeant handed over his driver's license and took the papers. "That's fine. Uh, I also need a neoprene case with a shoulder strap. I'll go with your recommendation on that one."

Rule Number Three: Deference is the most subtle form of flattery.

"Alrighty. And there's no transfer fee today." When Michael returned with the case, he said, "This pattern matches your outfit. Is that alright?"

"It's perfect."

"Is that all you need?"

"Where do you keep your ammunition? It looks like it could have went in that section over there," Philadelphia Sergeant said, pointing to a slew of empty shelves, "but I don't see any anywhere."

"We're actually out of stock on *all* ammo until December 2nd. Sorry about that."

"That's fine. There's always the internet."

Philadelphia Sergeant was filling out the forms. *Good. I won't have to worry about any wannabe heroes loading up one of these guns and shooting me in the back. This day was* made *for me...*

Out loud he said, "Michael, I think I'm finished."

"Okay, great! I'll need to see your ID, and I'll look these over," Michael replied, taking the papers back from his customer.

"That's fine. Take your time," Philadelphia Sergeant said as he reached into his chest pocket and pulled out his wallet. He was one hundred percent certain that there wouldn't be a problem. As an adult, he had never even been questioned by police.

While Michael was checking out the forms, Philadelphia Sergeant was silently singing. *A hunting I will go. A hunting I will go. Hi-ho the—*

Michael interrupted Philadelphia Sergeant's reverie, saying, "Well, everything appears to be in order. Let me ring you up."

"Alright. And I'll be paying in cash."

"No problem." Michael scanned the items, punched a few keys on the cash register and said, "Okay, for the gun and the camo case, that'll be $920.08."

Philadelphia Sergeant removed the money from his wallet and handed it to Michael without even counting it. That didn't go unnoticed.

Michael commented, "See you didn't need to count it. Must have known what you were buying before you came."

"I always do my research. I hate wasting time."

"Nothing wrong with that. Here's your change—79.92. And here's your box."

"Oh no, I don't need the box. I'll just put it in the case. I'll get the warranty info from Remington's website if there's a problem with it."

"You know your stuff, Kevin. Thank you for shopping at Walmart. Please come again. And thank you for the hunting lesson, too."

"Absolutely. Take care."

Phase one of his plan complete, Philadelphia Sergeant slung the gun case over his shoulder and marched off to the bathroom.

He received more than a few odd looks as he traversed the crowded aisles. Most South Philadelphians aren't used to seeing hunters in real life.

Under his breath, he said, "Hope the bathroom isn't crowded."

"Whatcha huntin'? It's about that time," an elderly white man said to him.

Not breaking his stride, Kevin hollered over his shoulder, "Whitetail!"

In his *mind* he said something totally different. *Blacktail. Blacktail monkeys. Flashy-dressing, loud-talking, fat, black monkeys.*

CHAPTER 11

WHILE THE JACKSON brothers were in the men's room grooming themselves in the long mirror to pass time, a young white man wearing a camouflaged outfit let out some kind of a high-pitched giggle as he walked by.

* * *

WALKING INTO THE men's room, Kevin had a mental pep rally. *This is it. No turning back now. Look at the monkeys dressed in red. Must be gangbangers; probably the* Bloods. *When I shoot 'em, I wonder if the blood on their clothes will be noticeable. Especially the chubby one. Hope he sticks around for the fireworks. It's going to be like shooting crabs in a barrel, or better yet, like shooting monkeys in cages!*

"*Tuh-hee!*" He didn't mean to laugh out loud. He was trying his best to contain himself.

* * *

*I*N A HUSHED tone, Terrell said to Malik, "Yo, you heard bouh? He *gotta* be throwed off. I ain't *never* hear a laugh like that, 'cept in psychopath movies. If he would've came in here skippin' and whistlin', I was out."

"I would've shot 'em. You *gotta* be a psycho walkin' 'round lookin' like that," Malik whispered back, and they both started laughing.

* * *

*L*OCKING THE DOOR to the stall, Philadelphia Sergeant hung his rifle on the hook, put a disposable seat cover on the toilet, pulled out his pistol, removed the silencer from his right cargo pocket, and sat down on the commode. He slowly threaded the homemade suppressor onto the modified barrel. He definitely wouldn't be winning any style points with his contraption.

Good for ten shots, he recalled. *Any more than that and the party's starting early.*

* * *

*M*ALIK BEGAN TO ask, "Yo, where your man—"

Terrell cut him off and hollered, "Ramos! Wassup Homie?!"

A short, red-haired Puerto Rican man wearing a blue *76ers* hoodie and tight-fitting designer jeans greeted the two brothers, "'Rell, Malik, what's good?"

Malik said, "Fly Ramos! Wassup?"

Ramos nodded and said, "We solid?"

Taking over the conversation, Terrell replied, "Absolutely. Soon as this dude roll out, then we can—"

A toilet flushed, and Terrell held up his index finger as if to say *Wait a minute*, then he nodded his head toward the stall.

* * *

*P*HILADELPHIA SERGEANT HAD taken the black disposable gloves out of his pocket and put them on. He stood up, flushed the toilet, wiped off the lock to the door, and slid the extra-long, silenced .40 caliber into his waistband.

He felt the cold metal of the can against the inside of his thigh. *Hope the gun doesn't fall. Stupid monkeys carry their pistols like this. Too cheap to buy a holster. Or too stupid.*

When Philadelphia Sergeant grabbed his rifle from the hook and slung it back over his shoulder, a switch flipped on inside of him. It was time for war. He felt like a heat-seeking missile locked onto the exhaust of an airplane. Nothing could deter him.

The Mossy-Oak-clad maniac unlatched the stall and noticed that the two gangbangers were still in there, now talking to a third party. *Probably trying to extort him.* Just a passing thought as he exited the bathroom with his gloved hands in his front pockets.

* * *

*T*HE CAMOUFLAGED MAN opened the stall's door, walked past the trio, and left the men's room.

Ramos said, "My dude ain't even wash his hands."

"I *told* you he was a psycho!" Malik exclaimed.

Terrell added, "*Dirty* white bouh. Whatever *he* 'bout to go hunt, I ain't eatin'." They all started chuckling, then in a quiet voice, Terrell said, "Ramos, take bouh stall. I'ma go in the one next to it."

The Jackson Brothers' final customer replied, "Got you," and went in to do the deal under the divider.

* * *

*A*S PHILADELPHIA SERGEANT made his way to the Control

Room, his brain continued to work. *This part of the mission* must *go off without a hitch. I hope this rifle isn't drawing too much attention. I would hate to be forced to modify my plan.*

Just be cool. No one has to die before I'm ready. I'm in charge. I'm as cold as ice and mean as a wolverine with a nagging wife. That's what Papa used to say...

* * *

*A*FTER THE TRANSACTION, Terrell said to Ramos, "Yo, we gonna leave out first. We been in this jawn long enough. Wait like thirty seconds. And you know I'm done, right?"

"Yeah, you told me. I can respect that."

"And I'ma line my youngin' up if he wit' it. I'll give him your handle so you don't dry up."[55]

"'Preciate you. Good luck, Homie."

"Thanks. Stay safe out there."

"And wash ya hands."

Terrell and Ramos burst out laughing.

---

[55] dry up – run out of drugs to sell

CHAPTER 12

*T*HE MANIAC WAS in the zone—muttering to himself. "Walk in, look right, shoot. Walk in, look right, shoot. Walk in, look right, shoot. Automatic. Hope that I only have to kill the monkeys. I'd hate to waste a white life. But they're all on the same side anyway.

"This is about *Mama*. I won't let any of them get away with this. If you're not with me, you're against me. And *none* of them were with me the day that Mama got trampled on. I'll fix 'em.

"Walk in, look right, shoot. Walk in, look right, shoot... " Philadelphia Sergeant was on autopilot.

The Control Room was constructed like a short alleyway. The left-handed door opened inward to a small room, rectangular like a high-end smartphone. There wasn't anything on the short walls of the room. Along the length of the two other walls were mile-long desks—one for each side—supporting numerous computer and CCTV monitors and four computer keyboards. In the center of the left-side desk was what appeared to be a keyhole.

The room was windowless, with just an exhaust fan, a louvered HVAC duct, and a sprinkler system in the ceiling.

There were four office chairs on the floor, but only three of them were occupied. Three people to contend with.

Philadelphia Sergeant was coming up to the gray nondescript door of the Control Room. Just one shopper seemed to pay him any mind. It didn't matter at this point. He was too invested.

Never breaking his stride, he drew the modified pistol from his waistband with his right hand, turned the doorknob with his left, stepped onto the black-and-white tiled floor of the Control Room, and fired one well-placed round as he let the spring-loaded door snap shut behind him.

The now-dead armed guard didn't even have time to blink. The subsonic bullet entered the man's forehead and instantly pulverized his brain. It seemed as though the guard went into a state of suspended animation—one hand on the grips of his sidearm, the other hand on the armrest thinking about pushing his body up out of the chair, his brown eyes forever gazing at the door.

The two other employees—loss prevention specialists—should have kept their faces glues to their monitors. Then they wouldn't have had to die afraid.

"No—" *POP-POP!*

"What are—" *POP! POP!*

It sounded like firecrackers. Not a big deal considering the extremely noisy atmosphere—TVs and sound systems blasting. But it wouldn't have mattered anyway. The entire Black Friday crowd was about to hear what was coming next.

Philadelphia Sergeant quickly unscrewed the hot silencer, wiped it off with his jacket, dropped it into a small wastebasket, and holstered his gun. He was glad to be rid of that monstrosity of a suppressor. Yes, it served a purpose, but he appreciated the terror caused by .40 caliber rounds at full volume—*if* it came to that.

Three seconds, three down. Right side, left side, right side. Three for three. Five shots. I'm on a roll. Only the first one had a gun. They didn't stand a chance.

"I have to lock it down. Right now. Then we can do some crowd control. I'm the Animal Patrol. Don't worry, Mama. I'll teach 'em good.

"Okay, I need the key. Where is the key? Where could it be?" he asked, at this point talking under his breath.

* * *

*A*S TERRELL AND Malik were walking away from the men's room, one of Malik's former clients—an attractive professional-looking woman now clean for thirteen months—eased up next to him and whispered, "I just seen a dude wit' a gun go in this side room near Layaway. I'm out."

Malik said, "Hold up. What you mean? What he look like?"

"White dude. Like he was goin' huntin'."

"He had a rifle on his back?"

"No. I mean, yeah, he had a rifle, but he pulled a pistol out his pants. And it looked like he had gloves on. Matter fact, he *did* have gloves on, 'cause his hands was dark."

"Crystal, you *sure*?"

"'Lik, I been clean over a year. I know what I saw. I'm out of here. *Y'all* can go tell somebody. I'm just givin' you a heads up. you lucky I saw *you*. I gotta go," she said, walking away at a good clip.

"Alright. Good lookin' out, Crystal!" Malik yelled to her back.

Ramos didn't acknowledge the brothers when he walked by. And he wasn't expected to. Discipline.

* * *

*U*NDER HIS BREATH, Russell said, "Alright, Princess, let me go find you some surprises."

He couldn't help but to smile. He loved his life. And he liked buying things, especially for other people.

CHAPTER 13

*P*HILADELPHIA SERGEANT LAID his rifle case against the far wall. He ran his gloved fingers along the undersides of the two desks. Nothing.

He checked the pockets on all three of the bodies. He didn't pull out anything that looked like it could fit into the cylindrical shaped keyhole on the console.

The madman was getting agitated. If he couldn't lock the doors, then he would have to alter his well-laid out plan. And time was flying. He already felt like he'd been in there for too long.

"The jackets," he breathed out. He searched the pockets of the three jackets hanging on the backs of the chairs, but to no avail.

Time was taunting his sick mind. Philadelphia Sergeant—control freak that he is—was close to losing it.

Then he looked at the dead guard's neck. A small silver chain glistened on his skin and disappeared underneath his shirt. "Bingo," the killer said out loud, and he snatched off the chain, key dangling in the air.

He dashed to the desk's center console, inserted the key, gave it a twist, opened up the clear dome, and hit the large red and yellow button. The words *ALL SECURE* popped up on the nearest monitor.

The state-of-the-art system was outfitted with electromagnetic mechanisms that slammed solid-steel tongues into place in every exterior door. If a particular entrance was ajar, the system was "smart" enough to wait until that door closed before firing its bolt.

As soon as Philadelphia Sergeant depressed the button, all of Walmart's entrances and exits simultaneously received the signal to lock. And *only* the Control Room's console could unlock them.

It took about thirteen seconds for the last of the doors to finally close and remotely bolt. Everything was exactly as the online schematics had depicted. Money well spent. *Tor* and *Bitcoin*—a criminal's best friends.

Now the killer could take his time. No one else could get in or out.

Philadelphia Sergeant walked to the back wall, unzipped his camo case, took out his Bushmaster, ejected and discarded the stock 10-round clip, reached into his left cargo pocket, pulled out a pair of taped magazines, slapped one into the assault rifle, and chambered a round. He got his earplugs out of one of the pouches on his belt and put them in.

Philadelphia Sergeant went over to the dead guard, pulled the man's Glock 23 from the holster, and tucked it into his own waistband.

He put his right hand on the doorknob to leave and his body went rigid. Then he smiled. He sauntered over to the left-side desk and removed the key. He said, "Can't forget this," slipped it into his chest pocket, and walked out.

Bushmaster in hand.

Safety off.

* * *

*T*HE RISING CACOPHONY of panic in the air was akin to slowly raising the temperature of the water while cooking a frog in a pot. The Jackson boys were oblivious to the signs of impending danger.

Standing in front of the indoor arcade, Terrell asked his little brother, "Yo, you think she was trippin'?"

"I don't know, Bro'. I doubt it," Malik replied. "I *know* Crystal. And if it's the same bouh from the bathroom, he definitely wasn't no cop. I might gotta take him out."

* * *

1557 FRIDAY 25 NOVEMBER 2022: *HUDAK*

*F*IRST, SHE SAW the gun come out of the door. Then, the strange-looking man who wielded it. The fearless blue-vest-clad associate manager said, "Hey, what were you doing in there?!"

Philadelphia Sergeant opened his eyes wide in feigned surprise, but said nothing.

The woman stepped closer. "Is th—"

BOOM-BOOM-BOOM-BOOM!

She never had a chance. The four bullets, traveling at over 2,000 feet per second, knocked the lady off of her feet, shattered her sternum, and shredded her heart and left lung. The associate manager was dead before she hit the floor. Dead even before she could ask, "Is that *blood* on you?!"

* * *

1557 FRIDAY 25 NOVEMBER 2022: *JACKSON BROTHERS*

"*W*HAT IS YOU *talkin'* 'bout?! We ain't cops, neither. That ain't our *job*. All we gotta do is dump the hammers and we good. We all the way done. We out. Game *over*. You must've bum—Yo, that's shots! That's somethin' big, man! We out!" shouted Terrell.

They weren't aware that the doors were already locked. And now it was complete chaos.

* * *

1557 FRIDAY 25 NOVEMBER 2022: *RUSSELL*

*R*USSELL WAS IN the toy section. *Zooma Kitty? Better than a* real *cat. Let me see what kind of batt—*

Shots rang out.

* * *

WOMAN SHOULD HAVE kept her Hispanic mouth shut, thought the madman as frightened screams filled the air.

And that sent him into a frenzy.

BOOM-BOOM-BOOM-BOOM-BOOM-BOOM-BOOM!

He shot his way to the Electronics department. Four more shoppers fell. Terrified people were scattering in all directions.

* * *

*M*ALIK GRABBED HIS brother's arm and asked, "What if somebody might need help, though?! What if I'm the only one in here wit' a burner?!"[56]

"You a *hero*, now?! You—Bro', they *still shootin'!* This might be our last chance to dip!"[57]

"We can't just run out on everybody! It's kids in here! Get low[58] and see wassup! Sooner we stop him, the better!"

"What about the cops?!"

"I ain't see none around here! Just the one car near Home Depot!"

The elder Jackson sighed. "*Wish* I would've brung my jawn in here. 'Lik, don't get me *shot*, man!"

"I got you! If we can make it to where the guns at, you can pick what you want!"

"*If.*"

---

[56] burner - gun

[57] dip - leave

[58] get low – take cover

* * *

*B*LACK CASHI—
  BOOM!
His impulsive trigger finger interrupted his train of thought.
Black cashier. Dead cashier. Me? One. Electronics? Zero. Actually, me? Four. Walmart? Zero.
It was like a video game in the sicko's head. Merciless.

Philadelphia Sergeant then took aim down a main aisle and let off eighteen more rounds in rapid succession, emptying the clip. About thirty bodies dropped. Half from the AR-15 and half from running and tripping over each other.

He ejected the magazine, flipped it over, slammed it back into the assault rifle, pulled the charging handle and said, "Two hundred ten to go," ever-mindful of his remaining ammo.

CHAPTER 14

*T*HE PIERCING SCREAMS of the shoppers were almost loud enough to muffle the sound of the gunfire.

"Dad, please let me make it home to my girls in one piece. Protect everybody else in here, too. And let whoever shootin' be stopped quick. Use me in whatever way You need to. In Yahshua's name I ask You this. Thank You," Russell prayed instinctively.

* * *

*P*HILADELPHIA SERGEANT WAS methodically picking off overweight black males—customers and employees—as he progressed through the aisles, his head on a swivel.

He didn't want to use more than two rounds per target. He planned to tally up as many casualties as possible. Dead or alive, blood was blood.

Budgeting bullets. Bullets on a budget. Have to budget my bullets. Says who? This is torture! I didn't know it would feel like this! I want to empty a clip into everybody! But you'll run out. So,

try to stick to the—
    BOOM-BOOM!
Double-taps and screams were the soundtrack of the hour. Percussion and vocals. Music to his sick ears.

* * *

*M*OMMY-BABY HAD the TV blasting. Judge Judy was one of her favorite shows. "... stop talking! I do not tolerate liars in my cour—"

"This is Fox 29 News and I'm Shaina Humphries. We're interrupting your programming for breaking news out of South Philadelphia. Details are sketchy at the moment, but we're receiving numerous reports of an active-shooter situation at Walmart on Delaware Avenue in the Pe—"

"No!" Mommy-baby's hand reflexively covered her own mouth. "Russell," she whispered.

She immediately prayed for her husband's safety and composed herself. *Okay, let me call him and make sure— But what if the shooter hears his phone ringing?*

Just then, her own phone sounded. It was a text message.

* * *

*C*ROUCHED DOWN IN a toy aisle with about sixty other shoppers, Russell decided to send his wife a quick text. It said:

    baby im in Walmart and im okay but somebody is shooting in here. cops were called. I'll be safe. call u when i can. turning my ringer off. love u

Russell didn't know what he was going to do, but he had to do *something*. There were so many women and children. He was getting angry. He just wanted to tell the whole store to stand back while he stopped this maniac.

Russell felt like he could outrun the pull of the trigger and take the madman to the ground—*without* killing him. Maybe he watched too many action movies. Maybe anger was clouding his judgment. Maybe—

BOOM!

That was like two aisles away!

AAH! HELP! NO!

BOOM-BOOM!

More terrified screams.

PLEASE! HELP M—

BOOM-BOOM! BOOM-BOOM! BOOM-BOOM! BOOM!

* * *

*E*VERYWHERE THAT HE walked, Philadelphia Sergeant left a trail of spent shell casings behind. With the Bushmaster pinned to his shoulder, he had a good rhythm going now—target a black male, squeeze the trigger, check his six, repeat. He was steadily working his way to the front of the store.

The madman shouted, "Why are you running?! There's nowhere to go! Fine! Run around, but it won't do you any good! Stupid monkeys! Do you know what you did?! You killed my mothe—"

The flash of a red jacket caught his attention. He swung the barrel of his rifle to the left.

BOOM-BOOM!

The bullets ripped into a man's upper back—right between the shoulder blades—and he hit the floor face first, almost doing a front flip.

"I told you that you can't run! *Look* at what happened to you!" screamed Philadelphia Sergeant while standing over the young black man that he had just cut down. He wondered why that red jacket seemed familiar and then he smiled. *The monkey from the bathroom.*

But he couldn't even savor the moment because of the noise. The screams were driving him crazy. "Shut up! Shut up!" he hollered at the top of his lungs. "Shut up, *please!*"

BOOM-BOOM-BOOM-BOOM-BOOM! BOOM! BOOM!

BOOM! BOOM! BOOM! BOOM!

Philadelphia Sergeant cleared a path to the main checkout area. Whoever fell, fell.

* * *

*A*S THE SHOOTER made his way to the front, the Jackson Brothers were making their way to the Sporting Goods department. They were like salmon swimming upstream—two determined men on an improbable mission.

"Yo, this bouh is crazy! He must got like a thousand shots! He ain't stoppin'!"

"And once we hit the gun section, *we* ain't stoppin'!" Malik hollered back at Terrell.

It seems like they weren't the only ones with payback on their minds. At least twenty other shoppers were arming themselves with pistols, rifles, and shotguns. They were preparing for war.

Terrell dashed to the broken handgun case and picked up a chrome Smith & Wesson .500—a monster of a revolver. It was so big that his pinky could fit inside of the barrel.

Malik told him, "'Rell, grab some shells and we out!"

Terrell yelled out, "Yo, somebody got some bullets they could spare? It ain't no more on the shelf!"

A man rounded the corner and shouted back, "There aren't any bullets at all! We're out of stock until next month!" It was Michael.

And upon hearing those words, the fight visibly went out of the small militia. To a man—and woman—they returned the weapons and scurried off seeking shelter.

Terrell turned to Malik and said, "Bro', what we gonna do? Look like you the only one wit' a gun."

"Ain't no *way* I'm the only one in this whole store!"

"Well, we ain't got time to go interview everybody! It's all on *you* for now. We gotta come up wit' a plan."

"We gonna have to split up first, so we can see where he at."

"So, if I spot him, then what?" asked Terrell

"Just, uh, text me and tell me where he at."

"Matter of fact, I could take flicks and send 'em to you."

"Yeah. *Yeah*, that'll work! Send a pic wit' a message wit' it."

"I'm on it."

"'Rell, be careful, Bro'. Bouh playin' for keeps."

"You ain't gotta tell *me* twice. I'm on stalk mode. And make sure you text *me* too, so I don't run into whatever it is he shootin'. That jawn sound like—"

The P.A. system blared to life.

CHAPTER 15

*A*T THE FRONT of Walmart—away from the shatter-resistant-but-not-bulletproof windows and doors—Philadelphia Sergeant shouted, "Shut up! Stop screaming and listen!"

He noticed a blue corded handset and ordered a teenaged employee to walk over to where he was standing. "Come here, come here, come here, come here! *You*, Sweetie! You work here. Come here. You're okay. I'm not going to hurt you. I just want you to show me how to use the intercom."

A pretty, heavyset young lady with cornrows, mocha skin, and tortoise-shell glasses reluctantly went over to the gunman and said, "Sure. Um, you just hit #-9-7 and speak into the mouthpiece."

"Speak up! Can't you see the earplugs?!"

"Oh! Yeah. Sorry. Um, hit #-9-7 and just talk," she said at a noticeably louder volume.

Hudak made the employee get his iPhone out of his pocket and told the frightened eighteen-year-old to record him.

"Uh, sir, I, um, I need your fingerprint to unlock it," she told him.

"Nice try. Use my face."

"*What?*"

"Use my *face!* Put the phone up to my face and it'll let you in!"

"Oh, I'm sorry! *Sorry!* I didn't know." The poor thing held the iPhone's screen up to the maniac's face, got access, took a few steps backward, and began recording.

No one else within the madman's field of vision dared to point a camera lens at him.

Wielding his AR-15 with one hand, Philadelphia Sergeant began, "Attention Walmart shoppers and employees! Shut up! Shut your mouths! Shut up! Shut up. Listen." He took control of the airwaves, and the noise level of the store actually dropped by about 20 decibels.

He had their attention. "Listen, I'm not going to kill *all* of you. I don't *want* to kill all of you. But I will if I have to.

"I have over seven hundred rounds of armor-piercing ammunition remaining. When that runs out, I'll remotely detonate some strategically placed bombs. Don't try to call my bluff. I've planned for every possible contingency.

"Think about it. I've successfully locked all of you inside of Walmart. I've taken one of the largest retail chains in the country hostage. Who would have thought that it was even possible?

"Becoming my prisoner was the last thing on your minds today. *I'm* in control. *I'm* the boss. Don't speak unless spoken to. Don't try to be a hero. If you're white, this isn't your fight. But if you try to get in my way, there's a bullet with *your* name on it, too.

"And just so you'll know, I've rigged my body with pressure-sensitive radio detonators linked to the bombs. So, if by some chance one of you *idiots* gets lucky enough to knock me to the ground, or even *touches* me in the wrong spot, the whole store's coming down on top of all of our bodies—or what's left of 'em."

The people had nowhere to go, and they were slowly starting to realize it. They began to hunker down. The bone-chilling cries and moans of the wounded and dying now filled the air.

One unlucky shopper was thinking, *First, I get shot at the Mummer's parade. Now, I'm the prisoner of a trigger-happy racist maniac. I'm a magnet for mass-shooters. I* wish *my husband was here.*

Mr. Hudak looked directly at the back of his phone and said, "Understand this: If I see *any* law enforcement trying to get in here, I will start executing *baby* monkeys. I mean it! This is *my* day! You do what *I* say!"

Looking back over the terrified crowd, the maniac said, "Listen up. I want to tell you a story: One year ago today, at this exact Walmart, a troop of black monkeys trampled my mother to death... "

A young African-American man's legs were beginning to cramp, so he decided to stand up and march in place. Wrong move.

Philadelphia Sergeant screamed, "Hey monkey! *You*, with the blue and white jacket! *Lay* down! I should blow your black head clean off for interrupting me! *Lucky* you're not fat or you'd already be bleeding out! That's *it*. If you move again, you're dead.

"Now, as I was saying—and turn off your ringers—Mama was only here to buy a new oven... "

* * *

JELANI, THE HOSTAGE wearing the blue and white jacket, was a tow truck driver for Triple A. He only came to Walmart to buy a sled for his five-year-old daughter.

Random thoughts raced through his mind. *Man, I just bought a new Durango. I ain't even get to show it to my brother yet...*

I don't want Yani' to grow up without a father. I better be careful...

How this happen in South Philly?! This can't be real. *All the shootin' these dudes be doin'?! I know* somebody *got a gun in here...*

Glad I ain't layin' in no blood. Is that selfish of me to think that right now?

All I got on me is a utility knife, but if I catch bouh sleepin'...

* * *

*T*HE KILLER WAS rambling on.

Refusing to become a victim again, Steve, a twenty-something year old Asian man who was standing in one of the aisles, devised a plan. He figured that he had a 97% chance of pulling it off. Better than a sitting duck's odds, for sure.

The throwing knives that his grandfather had given him—after a not-so-pleasant introduction to Philadelphia-after-dark—were tucked in the small of Steve's back. Five razor-sharp chances to end this nightmare.

The young man was deadly accurate from twenty yards out. With both hands. Once perfected, his one-two combination had never missed its mark. Eyes locked onto the target. Upward thrust of the left arm and a flick of the wrist, followed by an overhand right toss like a major league pitcher. Two blades traveling at the speed of light. Bullseye.

He just needed a clear line of sight. And twenty-four less feet between himself and the gunman. An 8-yard dash. Actually, more of a crawl. Slow and steady.

Crazy Man's distracted. This is my chance. My grandfather's going to be so proud of me. Steve slipped his hands underneath the back of his gray Temple Owls hoodie, and two matte-black carbon-steel knives were finally going to get to fulfill their purpose. One blade clutched between each set of thumb and forefinger.

A brown-skinned man sitting on the floor behind the hopeful hero wasn't too optimistic. *Really?! I* know *this bouh ain't about to throw no knife, man. He gonna get* everybody *shot.* A barely audible, "Yo" was being muttered over and over. It was the brown-skinned man trying to get Steve's attention. *This idiot ain't even turning arou—*

With the deliberation of a sloth, Steve began inching closer to the man with the guns. At the outset, Steve's movements were hardly noticeable, but with each step, he grew more emboldened. Not sloppy; just not as slow as before.

I don't know where he going, but 'least he ain't near me no more. Good luck, Jackie Chan, thought the man sitting on the ground formerly behind the man who was now trying to save the day.

The captives who saw what was transpiring grew hopeful. Maybe, just *maybe*, it would all be over soon.

*　*　*

*P*HILADELPHIA SERGEANT CONTINUED his diatribe. "... to the Electronics section for a stupid Playstation. That's why I shot that cashier in the face today. Anyway, this big buffalo monkey knocked me to the floor when I was trying to help Mama stan—Hey! You in the back by the meats!"

BOOM-BOOM-BOOM-BOOM-BOOM-BOOM-BOOM-snick.
Out of ammo.

In the blink of an eye, Philadelphia Sergeant dropped the blue handset and let it crash to the floor. He immediately drew his commandeered handgun and warned the crowd, "Don't even *think* about it!" He told his assistant, "Keep the camera on me! You're safe!"

With his eyes rapidly scanning from left to right and never looking away from his captive audience, he demonstrated his excellent hand-eye coordination. Using the same hand that was holding the pistol, he quickly released and caught the pair of magazines from his assault rifle, flipped them over, and slammed the full 30-rounder back into the Bushmaster. *What th—*

*　*　*

*T*HE CRAZY MAN was preoccupied. Steve saw his opportunity. And took it. Weaving in and out of his fellow shoppers and the occasional employee, the noble ninja was just about in range.

Steve's left shoulder tensed up; his front deltoid muscles were preparing to rotate his arm with enough torque to launch a 4-ounce projectile through the air at over 180 feet per second.

One more step and I got—
BANG-BANG-BANG!

* * *

*T*HE AUSTRIAN MADE Glock 23 barked death threats at a shopper who decided to take a step too close toward Hudak. The supersonic .40 caliber jacketed hollowpoints splintered the Asian man's left humerus, causing him to howl in agony.

The man's black knives hit the floor hard, but the killer didn't even notice due to the terrified chorus of voices. That was fortunate for the ninja with the bullets in his arm; better than his brain. The gunman definitely would have made an example out of him to discourage any other wanna-be heroes.

Philadelphia Sergeant's instincts were sharp. But firing his gun when he did was just dumb luck. He had no idea of how close he actually came to a fatal case of lead poisoning.

"Shut up and calm down!" the gunman yelled as loud as he possibly could. "This is over when *I* decide! *I* have the gun! *I* run the sh—"

A can of Pepsi soared through the air and hit the floor, exploding about four feet to the left of the maniac, showering him with soda.

The store—well, everyone who saw what had just happened—collectively gasped.

Mr. Hudak said to his 18-year-old assistant, "Dear, please get the handset and hold it up so that I can speak. Hold the iPhone back a little bit with your other hand. There you go."

She resembled an archer about to release an arrow at her target.

In a voice barely above a whisper and building up to a shout, the lunatic said, "I see that I'm not being taken seriously. I guess that the blood and bodies covering the floor aren't enough incentive for you ignorant monkeys to cooperate!"

In a flash, Philadelphia Sergeant dropped the handgun into his pants pocket and yanked the charging handle on the AR-15, chambering a round. Another collective gasp filled the air.

"Excuse me, ma'am" he said, motioning to a light-skinned African American woman wearing a multi-colored scarf. My mother was almost your age when she was murdered. Come here, please."

The woman stood up tall and said, "I don—"

BOOM!

The scarf was yanked off of the back of her head by the departing fragments of skull and brain matter and bullet.

The people didn't know *what* to do.

"Hey, Dear, I'll take the handset. You just step back and keep recording. Thank you," he said to his assistant who was visibly shaking.

"You weirdo! You creep!" a shopper yelled from behind an aisle.

Philadelphia Sergeant was fed up. Through the handset he shouted, "Shut up! Listen up! I'm—Hey, cut the camera off! That's enough! Post the video to CBS' social media. Now!"

The teenaged girl fumbled with the phone and almost dropped it. "Okay, okay. I did it," she said, attempting to hand him back his iPhone.

"No! Put it in my left cargo pocket and go over there!" he said, pointing to the right with the barrel of his assault rifle. That gesture made everyone in that direction duck down.

"Calm down! Calm down. I'm going to let *some* of you leave. *If* you try to run, or if this turns into another stampede, I'll just mow everybody down. So listen up.

Everyone who is *not* of African descent—and I *do* have eyes. If you try to trick me, you will die. Everyone who is *not* black, or *half*-black, *slowly* begin to make your way to the Health & Beauty section.

"If there are *any* monkeys—male or female—*in* the Health & Beauty section, get out of there *now*. No running, no pushing. *Order*.

"All women monkeys *over* forty-five years of age, and all monkey children *under* eighteen years of age—regardless of who you came in here with—make your way to the Lawn & Garden section. Don't run. If a child is too young to go alone, one of you other monkeys had better take them with you," he threatened.

As the younger children were forced to leave their fathers and mothers and cousins, aunts, and uncles; crying was breaking out all around the store.

Over the P.A. system, a soothing voice said, "It's okay little ones. Everything is going to be okay. Don't cry. It's okay. It's alright."

It was Hudak. He was completely out of his mind.

He started again, "Now listen up. If I did *not* assign you to a section, there's a chance that you might die today. You might be thinking that I can't kill all of you. Actually, I *can*. But I don't want to. No. I want to see some of you go back to whatever jungle it is that you came from, and tell the rest of your primate family about what happened here today.

"You're free to go and hide now—don't *run*—and if you're still breathing when the doors open, you made it.

"If *anyone* tries to attack me in *any* way, you will most certainly be put down like a rabid dog.

"For those of you I *did* assign to a section: Once the hunting begins, if any desirables enter your area for asylum, I'll probably toss a frag' grenade in that direction—no need to waste ammo, right? And I'll just chalk you up as collateral damage. So, it would be to your advantage if you didn't let them in. But that's up to you."

CHAPTER 16

*T*ARA JOHANNSEN WAS in her bedroom trying on some new outfits, with her television playing low in the background. She really wanted to look good for her boyfriend tonight.

Ms. Johannsen *had* been taking advantage of Kevin, keeping his car for as long as she wanted to. She didn't care about any prior obligations that Kevin may have had. And that wasn't right.

Tara also felt guilty for cheating on him for several months. She even had her illicit lover in Kevin's car for the first time, a few days ago. Not to mention that she actually set up her supplier to get robbed. What was she *thinking?* It was time for all of that to come to an end. Man-Man wouldn't like it, but he didn't own her, so, oh well.

Tara just wanted to start fresh. She could sense a slight rift developing between herself and Kevin, and she didn't want that. She really cared for him.

So, what if they had different tastes in music and movies? That wasn't a deal-breaker, not by a long shot. Kevin was independent, smart, funny, boy-band attractive, and *dependable*. She could always count on him.

So, why wasn't he answering her calls or responding to her texts? Maybe he was still mad at her from earlier. She would definitely make it up to him tonight.

She changed the channel to CBS to see if anything interesting was happening. A commercial was on, so she sat in front of her mirror trying out different shades of lip gloss. Lost in deep thought, she didn't notice that the broadcast had resumed, but when the news anchor said the words, "alleged gunman," Tara's head automatically whipped around to the television. Her eyes were glued to the screen.

* * *

1618 FRIDAY 25 NOVEMBER 2022: *CBS BROADCAST CENTER*

"... *C*HANNEL 3 CBS Eyewitness News at 4. I'm Janelle Burrell, and we have breaking news out of South Philadelphia. At approximately 3:45 p.m., we began to receive numerous reports of an active shooter at a Walmart on Delaware Avenue. We now have more information.

"A mass-shooting has been confirmed through multiple cellphone videos and pictures from the shoppers and employees trapped inside.

"It has now been declared an official hostage situation, and there are dozens of casualties. Law enforcement is on the scene, and they are currently doing everything that they can to bring this crisis to an end.

"Our producers are preparing the video clips and photos for broadcasting. We've received hundreds of files, but much of the footage is too graphic for our viewing audience.

"This—hold on... We've actually received what may be a video from the alleged gunman himself... My producers are going to put it on the air in a few moments. They want me to advise you that it may be difficult to watch. Please excuse the language... "

* * *

"*WHAT?!* NO!" TARA screamed out loud.

This *couldn't* be right. She was watching a video of her *boyfriend*, dressed in hunting gear—with *blood* on his sleeves—holding an assault rifle and admitting to *killing* people. And he was shooting guns on *camera!*

Am I high?! *Was that not just Kevin on TV? Why didn't they say the name? What if they don't know that it's him? I'm not saying anything; they might try to implicate* me. *But they can't. I didn't know anything about this; I didn't even know that Kevin was capable of* doing *something like this!*

I need to get out ahead of this. I'm not going to jail for anybody! *I'll call the news people. No! They'll want a story or something. I'm calling the cops. Know what? I don't care. I'm calling them all. I'm innocent!*

Although the iPhone video didn't show any actual victims, the crazed gunman's rhetoric chilled many viewers to the bone and enraged countless others.

South Philadelphians began to show up to Walmart in masses.

* * *

*A*FTER LISTENING TO the madman's speech for a while, Terrell said, "Yo, bouh is out of control! This don't even sound *real*."

"Yeah, well 'least we know where he at. For now."

"Right. But if we try to catch him up there, he *definitely* gonna see us comin' and start choppin' at us. We gotta wait 'til he start movin' again."

"Ain't no doubt. We might as well get in position now, so we could box him in like a queen and a rook."

"Chess. I like that. Let's do it."

"But hold up. What about the pressure jawn? If he hit the ground, we *all* cooked."

"Man, dude *lyin'*. You seen him in the bathroom. Ain't no *way* he could've brung all that in here! And I ain't never even hear about no detonator like that in the *movies*. Bouh fraudin',[59] Bro'. He ain't tryin' to blow nothin' up. He a *shooter*."

"Me too."

The two brothers shoulder-hugged and went their separate ways. From this point on, the Jackson boys communicated strictly via images and text.

---

[59] fraudin' - lying

CHAPTER 17

*P*HILADELPHIA SERGEANT FELT a tingling sensation on his thigh and spoke into the blue handset. "The girl that I gave my iPhone to, come here please. I am *not* going to hurt you at all. Please come here. My phone is vibrating."

When the young lady arrived, the killer said to her, "Please pull out my left earplug, and put the phone on speaker and hold it for me."

The poor girl almost went for the wrong plug. A barely perceptible arm movement. The amounts of fear and stress that she felt were off the charts. *His left*, she reminded herself, and then pulled it out with her right hand. Finally, she hit the speakerphone icon and took a half step back on wobbly legs.

"Hello? This is the Crisis Negotiator for the Philadelphia Police Department. Who am I speaking with? Hello?" said the iPhone.

With his eyes still glued to the hostages—and finger on the trigger—the gunman answered, "Yes? What can I do for you?"

"What is your name, sir?" the negotiator asked him.

"My name isn't important. I'm sure that you've seen the footage.

Did you catch my warning about what will happen if you try to come in?"

"Yes. Loud and clear. How many people are hurt? We have paramedics standing by, ready to assist the woun—"

"I'm not falling for that! As soon as I unlock the doors, you guys will come flooding in! The doors will be opened when *I'm* ready!"

"What do you want?"

"I want my mother back! I want a confession and an apology from the monk—"

"Sir, I can't give you that. I am—"

"I *know* that! I'm not stupid! Here are my demands: I want all law enforcement to reposition themselves one hundred yards away from every entrance and window.

"I want a Greyhound bus. Tinted windows. Veteran driver with ID. Gas tanks full; I know that there are two of 'em. Fill 'em up. I want my bus by 5:30. Not hard to get.

"No tricks. Anyone tries to come in, and I'm killing infants and seniors *first*. Then, I'll detonate some bombs. I planted eight of 'em. Kill me and you'll kill everybody else, too.

"At 5:30, I get on the bus. You don't follow me. Fifteen minutes into my ride, I'll call you to tell you where the bombs are.

"5:30 sharp, or I'll start killing *white* women. I'll save the monkeys for last. Don't call me; I'll call you." Philadelphia Sergeant instructed his assistant to disconnect the call and put the phone back into his pocket.

Before the bus gets here, I'll have to shave and change clothes. I'll open the doors at five. Then I can walk out with the rest of the shoppers. That's how they fooled that monkey Denzel in Inside Man. *But first—*

BOOM-BOOM-BOOM-BOOM-BOOM-BOOM-BOOM!

He unleashed a barrage of bullets about five feet above the heads of the hostages in one of the main aisles.

"—I got me some monkeys to kill!" he shouted, but his words were drowned out by the screams of the terrified captives.

He planned to start at the back of the store and work his way forward, pocketing a few items along the way in preparation for his great escape. But unbeknownst to Kevin Hudak, his name was now plastered all over the news, thanks to his new *ex*-girlfriend. In this "woke" climate, silence was treason.

* * *

SINCE 4 P.M., the news broadcast had Man-Man's attention. He *lived* for drama. Every time that he saw a red and white *Breaking News* notification flash across a TV screen, his heart would race.

But this was different. This was happening in South Philly. To black people. People that he probably knew. His blood boiled.

I wish *I would've been in there. Bouh wouldn't be makin' no videos; I know* that *much.*

How nobody *in there got no burner though? That don't even make no sense. And this nut dude, man. He wearin' a* leaf—

Man-Man's thoughts were interrupted by two words. "... Kevin Hudak."

He jumped up off of his couch. "Didn't I see that name on—Hey, yo!" He called Tara *immediately.*

When she answered the phone, she was crying.

Man-Man asked, "That's *him*, ain't it?!"

Sobbing, Tara admitted, "Yeah, but I didn't know anything about this! I'm *serious*, Man-Man! I'm not like that! He's sick! What's wrong with him?! He could've *killed* me! I slept in the bed with him! I didn't know that he had *guns!*" Tara's pitch grew higher and higher.

She sounded as if she were going to hyperventilate, so Man-Man cut in, saying, "Hey. Hey, Tee. I know it ain't your fault. Some cats is good at hidin' stuff. How could you know? You couldn't. I know you ain't into that. Don't lose your mind over that weirdo, alright? For real."

"Okay," Tara said, taking a deep shaky breath. Then she asked him, "Can you pick me up?"

"*Now* I get to come to your spot. I'm on my way."

Some guys have all the luck.

CHAPTER 18

*A*S FRIGHTENING AS the Walmart massacre had been up to this point, it now seemed as though every horror movie villain that had ever been created was unleashed on the captives, judging by the way that they were screaming.

They knew that the end was coming, but they didn't know what *kind* of end it was going to be.

And that's what scared them.

Why didn't he shoot anyone? And where is he going? Is he...skipping?

Once Philadelphia Sergeant passed all of the aisles and reached the rear of Walmart, he was all business. Step by silent step, he scouted for targets. It wasn't hard, because all of the people that he didn't want to kill were already out of the way.

Open season on prime monkey.

He was uncharacteristically quiet. The only thing that gave away his position was the sound of the AR-15 erupting every so often.

Even the running and hollering had died down. The captives were hoping that their stillness and silence would render themselves invisible. Of course, the one force able to snap them out of their statuesque trance was the sight of the gunman.

But the wounded didn't even care. If help didn't arrive soon, they would be dead anyway.

Philadelphia Sergeant grew weary of letting his quarry see him coming, so he made up a new game. As he walked through an aisle—ignoring the whimpering prey—he'd pause several feet before an upcoming intersection, then he would take a few quick steps and make an abrupt ninety degree turn to the right or to the left.

The looks on the monkeys' frightened faces were priceless. When they saw Philadelphia Sergeant and his big black Bushmaster turn the corner, it was—*BOOM-BOOM!*—already too late.

Some people ignored his warning about seeking refuge in the off-limit areas, but the gunman's empty threat had produced the intended effect. He had managed to turn the captives against one another.

Rule Number Four: Deception can be mightier than the sword.

Whenever an undesirable tried to run into a safe zone, that person was immediately met with shouting and shoving, or punches and kicks. If the former wasn't effective, then the latter *never* failed.

No one wanted to risk getting blown apart by a grenade. One incident in particular was downright cruel.

A young black man with a light mustache and box haircut, wearing a pair of black jeans and a black satin Las Vegas Raiders jacket, tried to run into the Lawn & Garden section to escape the wrath of the gunman.

A rather large and solidly built woman with short hair and mocha skin stiff-armed the smaller intruder in the chest, and another hostage—a 14-year-old boy—punched him in the mouth.

The smaller intruder stumbled backwards, and then he started to approach the same aisle again.

The large lady kicked at him and hollered, "Ain't no grown men back here! Don't get yourself hurt worse! You better find somewhere else to go!"

"But I'm a woman! I had gender reassignment!" the determined asylum seeker shouted, the blood from her lips turning her teeth a deep crimson.

"Tell it to the crazy man!"

"Look, I'm tellin' you the truth! I can prov—"

"Ain't no young *women* back here, either! You ain't gonna get *us* all blown up! Find somewhere else to *go!*" the large woman yelled as she half-choked and half-pushed the smaller lady away for the last time.

GET OUT OF HERE!

The hostages weren't taking any chances.

The authorities felt helpless. Even from outside of Walmart they could hear the gunman's assault rifle exploding at random intervals, but they didn't know if it was purely for intimidation, or if the madman was actually killing more people.

How many rounds did he have?

The store was huge, and that gave people hope. But the store was jam-packed, and that made Philadelphia Sergeant smile.

He kept himself entertained as he navigated the aisles. *I only have about three mags left, plus however many rounds are in my pistols. If I take it slow and kill maybe two monkeys per aisle, that should easily take me to check-out time.*

This is too easy. It doesn't even seem fair. The only resistance that I encountered was a can of soda. Spineless monkeys—only tough when they *have the guns. The General is going to be so proud of me. I—*

He turned right and saw a dark-skinned man kneeling on the hard floor, already in the perfect position for an execution. That's what Hudak thought, and—*BOOM-BOOM!*—that's what Hudak did.

He was on the hunt. But so were Terrell and Malik. Little did the madman know, but with each double-tap, the Jackson brothers were closing in on him.

After listening to the changing proximity of the gunfire for a few minutes, Terrell sent the first text message. It read:

i think he working his way to the front of the store

Malik sent a two-word reply:

got you

Upon further careful observation and some stealthy repositioning, Terrell took a gamble. He thought that he saw the shooter pause for a few seconds before exiting out of each row. He sent a text to Malik that read:

yo i think he gonna be near the bedding aisles. try to get close to there. i got a idea. get back to u soon.

Malik sent back:

alright give me a minute

The younger Jackson had to come all the way from the other side of the store.

In the meantime, Terrell crept to the Bedding aisle closest to the Electronics department, and he laid prostrate on the floor. In the next aisle ahead, he saw a guy with the neon green hat holding some kind of a cloth on a man's upper thigh.

Something clicked in Terrell's mind. *That look like the same bouh that let me go through the stop sign. I remember that dumb hat. That's wassup, though. He always lookin' out for somebody. Hope he don't get shot.*

The older Jackson snapped a picture of what was in front of him, and he started typing. The message that he sent read:

im on the floor in bedding. take the big aisle over here and stop right past the craft supplies but make sure you can't see in my aisle.

After a few moments, Malik successfully completed the journey. He took a picture and sent a message with it that said:

aight I think im here

Terrell looked at the image on his screen and replied:

good. thats perfect. when crazy dude walk past me he gonna stop near the end of my row. soon as he do ima push him to the middle of the intersection. u know what to do.

Malik shot back:

> *text me soon as he get to your row. I got a idea. he probably gonna try to creep up on me*

Terrell wrote:

> *but what about me pushing him*

Malik responded:

> *still push him when he stop. ima just make sure he stop. trust me bro. and make sure u text me soon as u see him*

Terrell agreed:

> *alright be careful*

Malik replied:

> *u be careful. im the one with the gun*

Then the younger Jackson drew his pistol and motioned for everyone in the immediate area to get *out* of the immediate area. *Immediately.*

The wait didn't take long. The whimpers of the hostages betrayed the killer's presence, and Terrell sent two words:

> *he here*

Malik almost couldn't breathe. But he pulled himself together enough to stick to the plan.

Around the corner and to Terrell's right, a man's voice could be heard saying, "If this racist clown mom could see this, she'd roll over in the grave. She'd probably say, 'Look at the *idiot* I raised. Stupid redneck boy ain't learn *nothin'*. You don't dress like no hunter in the city... "

Terrell could hear his brother trying to commit suicide. *'Lik! What are you doin?!*

With his earplug still dangling, Hudak crept past the prone Terrell, feeling like something wasn't quite right. *I shot the monkey with the red jacket in a different part of the store, so how could I have just walked past him? I'll figure that out later. Right now, I have more pressing matters to attend to, like shooting the mouth off of this fool around the corner.*

Hudak checked his six and stopped right before the end of the bedding aisle. Listening. *Itching* to blow monkey brain all over the shelves.

Malik—gun in hand—could now be heard saying, "... wonder what kind of mom *she* had to be to raise up a racist hillbilly. Probably *good* that she dead... "

Hudak heard enough.

But so did the man with the red jacket.

Terrell M. Jackson was 6'2" and 225lbs of solid muscle. He was one of the select few who continued their prison workout regimens on the street. He never skipped a training session. Malik's big brother was fast and extremely strong.

But Hudak was no pushover, either. Especially with that big black Bushmaster, a bad attitude, and vengeance on his mind.

As discretely as a large man wearing a red jacket could, Terrell pushed himself up off of the floor, never fully standing, and took off, closing the distance between himself and the shooter in less than a second.

It was all or nothing.

Terrell threw his shoulder into the middle of Hudak's back with all of his might. The gunman sailed deep into the intersection but managed to stay on his feet.

Terrell tried to stop himself short of the converging aisles, but the floor was already slick with blood. He slipped and went down hard.

As Hudak swung around with his Bushmaster at the ready, he saw a flash of red from a man's vest. *The mon—*

Gunfire erupted.

BANG-BOOM!

BANG!

BANG-BANG-BANG-BANG-BANG-BANG-BANG-BANG-BANG!

The first bullet tore into his shoulder.

The second bullet went wild and lodged itself in the ceiling.

The third bullet broke Philadelphia Sergeant's neck, severing the top of his spinal cord and sending shards of C-1 vertebrae into the base of his brain. He crumpled to the floor like a puppet with its strings cut.

The next nine bullets were wasted on an already dead body.

It was over.

If the dead man would've had time to complete his thought, it would have been, *The monkeys from the bathroom!*

But time wasn't on his side.

CHAPTER 19

"*H*E DEAD! HE dead! They got him! He dead y'all! We safe! It's over!" shouted Russell. He saw it all unfold.

Word began to spread throughout the store.

The manager of Walmart also happened to be nearby, and he ran up to the Jackson brothers and said, "The key! He has the key on him! It unlocks the doors! People are still dying! We have to find the key!"

Malik and Terrell quickly rolled Hudak's lifeless, bullet-riddled body onto its back, squatted down, and began rifling through the endless pockets.

"I think I got it. This it?" asked Malik, handing the oddly-shaped key to the pudgy manager with the ruddy face.

"Yup, that's it! Thank you both! I have to open up these doors! See you soon!" the manager told the Jackson brothers, and he was off.

Rushing through the gray nondescript door, the manager was taken aback by the sight in the Control Room—blood and bodies belonging to people he once knew.

The man gagged and then vomited on the floor. He couldn't even make it to the wastebasket.

He wiped his mouth with the back of his hand, sucked in a few deep breaths, and took a moment to gather himself. "Okay, let's make this quick," he said out loud.

The manager raced to the desk's console, inserted the key, turned it to the *ACTIVE* position, lifted up the dome, and hit the big red button. The word *UNSECURED* flashed across one of the monitors, and the manager got out of there as fast as he could, leaving the key right where it was.

But while the store manager was making his way to the Control Room, Malik and Terrell embarked on a mission of their own.

Aware of the overwhelming police presence right outside of the doors, and knowing that he would immediately go back to prison if found in possession of a firearm, Malik turned to his brother and said the only logical thing that a criminal could say in the heat of the moment. "Yo, I gotta get rid of this burner, ASAP."

"Where you gonna dump it at?" Terrell asked a worried Malik.

"If I hide it in the back of a shelf somewhere, somebody gonna end up findin' that jawn."

"You could put it wit' the rest of the guns."

"Sportin' Goods. We out."

For some reason, the store was still crowded. And excessively noisy.

The Jackson brothers thought that the survivors would have been pouring out of every exit by now. What was the hold up? Didn't really make a difference. Once they got rid of the gun, it was *Adios Amigos*.

On the way to the Sporting Goods department, Terrell snatched a novelty T-shirt from a display table, gave it to Malik and said, "For the prints. But wait 'til we get there."

"Ain't no doubt," replied Malik.

"And your shells was clean, right?"

"*Always.*"

Upon arriving at the firearm section, the younger Jackson quickly walked over to the handgun case, pulled the 9mm Kel-Tec pistol from his pocket, ejected the magazine, wiped them both down with the borrowed shirt, reinserted the clip, and hid the gun that killed the monster among a pile of other semi-automatics.

Malik and his brother never even *thought* about celebrating. To them, this was just one more chapter in a life filled with drama. It was time to get home.

They had just cleared the Electronics department when a police officer stopped them.

CHAPTER 20

*T*HE DOORS OPENED up unexpectedly, and the former hostages started pouring outside. They were ordered to get on the ground by law enforcement as the authorities rushed in.

Almost immediately, the survivors began to shout, "The shooter's dead! He's dead! Let us go!"

It was a stalemate.

The police couldn't release anyone until they found out exactly what happened. Fortunately, it didn't take long.

The store manager identified himself and told a hulking African American SWAT sergeant about the two young men who killed the shooter. The manager mentioned that they had found the override key in the gunman's pocket, and that's how they were able to unlock the entrances. He even gave the exact location of where the gunman's body could be found.

The sergeant passed the information up the chain of command, and the survivors were finally free to leave or to seek medical attention in the triage area set up in front of Walmart. A number of EMTs were allowed to enter the store in order to assess who needed immediate care or immediate transport, and several bomb-sniffing dogs were escorted in by their handlers.

* * *

*U*NBEKNOWNST TO CIVILIANS, there was a BOLO out for the Jackson brothers. They were wanted for questioning. All that the police had was a description, but that was good enough.

The color red was easy to spot.

"Excuse me, gentlemen, are you the two men who killed the shooter?" the uniformed police officer asked Malik and Terrell as they were walking away from the Electronics section.

Malik quickly spoke up, "Yeah, that was us, but we ain't lookin' for no fame or nothin'."

The officer took out a notepad and an ink pen and said, "Hold up a minute. Can I have your names, please?"

"Malik Jackson, and my brother name Terrell Jackson." *Man, I should have said it's not* us. *I'm trippin'.*

"No kidding? Two brothers? You can't make this stuff up. Do you still have the gun on you?"

"Naw, I ain't got it no more."

"Where is it?"

"I don't know. I don't know what I did after that. I'm still kinda in shock."

"Well, listen guys. I have a detective in the breakroom who needs to get an official statement from you, then you can probably go home, get some rest. Sound good?"

Terrell finally opened his mouth. "Lead the way."

There were two detectives, both dressed in black blazers and almost identical light blue shirts, sitting at a table in the breakroom.

The suit with the bald head and dark complexion began, "Gentlemen, why don't you join Mr. Rosado and I? Have a seat."

After passing off his notes, the uniformed police officer stayed in the room, leaning on a wall by the door.

The dark-skinned detective continued, "First and foremost, I would like to thank you men for putting your lives on the line and taking down a dangerous killer."

"You welcome," the Jackson brothers replied in unison.

The dark detective hit the red button on the recorder and began his interrogation. "For the record, can you please state your names?"

"Malik Jackson."

"Terrell M. Jackson."

"And were you both in Walmart during the attack?"

"Yes."

"Yes."

"The man that you killed, did you see him with a gun?"

"Yes."

"Yes."

"Was he the man responsible for shooting the customers and employees?"

"Yes."

"Yes."

"And how did you stop the gunman?"

Terrell answered first this time. "I pushed him in his back hard, right into a open area—"

"And I shot him," Malik finished.

The detective resumed his questioning. "Malik, where did you get the gun?"

"From the Sportin' Goods counter." The younger Jackson lied effortlessly.

"Can I see the gun?"

"I ain't got it no more."

"Where is it?"

"Like I told the other officer, I don't know. I'm still kinda in shock."

"So, you don't know what you did with the gun after you shot the man? Did you put it in your pocket? Did you put it on a shelf? Did you give it to someone else?"

"I think I put it on a shelf."

"And then what did you do?"

"Uh, the manager ran up to me and said that we need to find the key for the doors. So that's what we did. We checked him and got the key out his pocket, and the manager went to open up the doors."

"Did you see anyone take the gun from the shelf?"

"I doubt it."

"Either you did or you didn't."

"No, I ain't see nobody. But we ain't stand there. We left."

"So, you mean to tell me that you remember all these other details, but when it comes to the gun that you used to kill a *terrorist*, you have no idea what happened to it?"

"It could st—"

"We stopped him! You treatin' us like *we* the criminal!" Terrell hated seeing his baby brother getting grilled like that.

The salt-and-pepper haired Detective Rosado broke his silence saying, "Calm down, sir. It's standard procedure when a weapon is involved. And we'll need to see both of your ID's."

Terrell kept it up. "Do we need a lawyer, too?!"

"Just your IDs, sir. Please don't raise your voice."

As the Jackson brothers retrieved their driver's licenses, the bald-headed detective noticed a yellow card in each one of their wallets and asked, "Are both of you on parole?"

"Yeah," they answered in unison again.

"And you drove here?'

"Yeah, I did," groaned Terrell. He knew the routine.

The bald detective continued to question Terrell. "What kind of vehicle do you have?"

"A silver Honda Accord."

"Where are you parked at?"

"Right out front. First row, closest to Home Depot."

Mr. Rosado cut in again and said, "I'll need your keys," and when Terrell handed the fob over, the detective tossed it to the uniformed officer who then immediately left the room.

About ten minutes later, a call came over the detectives' radios. They found Terrell's gun. And $3,500.00 cash.

The Jackson brothers were handcuffed without incident and allowed to sit back down.

Detective Rosado had retrieved a thick wad of bills from Terrell's pocket, and he plopped it down onto the table. "So, where do you boys work?"

Silence.

The dark-skinned investigator sent for the store manager via two-way radio. When he showed up, the bald lawman told him, "We'll need to view your CCTV footage." He turned to Mr. Rosado and asked, "Can you stay here with these two?"

Detective Rosado replied, "No problem."

It didn't take long to piece together. There was only a small block of time that the authorities had to focus on. And the color red was easy to track.

The investigator and another officer huddled around a monitor in the Control Room—ignoring the dead bodies and blood and vomit—and watched as the two Jackson brothers walked to the Sporting Goods department right after handing the manager the key.

Malik reached into his pocket, wiped off a compact gray and black handgun, and slipped it into the broken display case.

"Got you," the dark-skinned detective mumbled.

CHAPTER 21

*T*HE MAN WITH the green hat, as he came to be known, was carrying a wounded African American guy through Walmart's writhing human labyrinth like one would carry a new bride across the threshold. "You're gonna be okay," Russell assured the lethargic man in the bloody Raiders jacket. Only the right sleeve was soaked. *Probably shot in the shoulder or upper arm. He'll make it.*

Miraculously, Russell had managed to avoid detection, and he was able to stash a number of the injured in different spots throughout the store so that they wouldn't get trampled on in the utter chaos.

Every area that the shooter vacated, the man with the green hat ran to, looking for the wounded.

Russell was returning from one of his caches just now, intending to transport the bleeding man to his truck. Oh, how he adored that truck.

But he put people first every time.

The parking lot was a nightmare. First responders—paramedics and law enforcement—occupied the first thirty yards directly in front of the store. Firetrucks held down the periphery. There was also a temporary blood bank erected by the Red Cross. And the various news vehicles posted up where they could.

Healthy survivors were anxious to get home. Traffic was trying to move in all directions. But amazingly—especially for South Philadelphians—no one was blowing a horn or being rude.

The main entrance to Walmart was just as hectic as the parking lot. EMTs were attempting to wheel stretchers in and out; an untold number of police were shuttling back and forth; the walking wounded were trying to leave; and Good Samaritans were entering the store in order to help those who couldn't walk, even wheeling the victims out in shopping carts.

There were just way too many critically injured people for law enforcement to worry about well-meaning civilians disturbing the crime scene. Saving lives was the number one priority.

On the way to his pickup, Russell walked behind a female reporter from Channel 6 who was giving a play-by-play of the aftermath.

"... and I'm Katie Katro here at Walmart on Delaware Avenue in South Philadelphia, the location of a tragic mass-shooting, reporting live on the massive rescue effort. We don't have a figure for the number of casualties at this time, but we do have confirmation that the alleged gunman, Kevin Hudak, has been killed.

"There are a number of bomb-sniffing dogs in the store attempting to locate any potential explosive devices that the gunman may have planted. As you would expect, it is complete pandemonium down here by the Delaware River... "

Key fob already in hand, Russell pushed the button to unlock his doors. With the guy still cradled in his arms, he managed to get two fingers on the front-passenger door's handle and pull it open.

After depositing the man onto his seat—his truck was the perfect height; he didn't have to bend over—and carefully shutting the door, his mind was still on overdrive. *Well, at least I was finished shopping before the Sabbath started. And Yahshua said that it's lawful to do good on the Sabbath, so this is absolutely fine.*

I got time for one more passenger, and I can put him in the bed if I can get something soft for him to lay on.

I better hurry up. Oh yeah, let me text the wife and tell her that I'm okay.

But as soon as he pulled out his phone, Russell received a message of his own. From Mommy-baby. It read:

> *i see that ur ok. when i saw a man with a ugly green hat carrying somebody, i knew that it was u! call me when u can. love u! halleluyah!*

Russell jogged back to the entrance, passing behind that same reporter again. As the man with the green hat entered the store, Terrell and Malik were being escorted out by the police.

Russell made eye contact with the brothers and mouthed the words *Thank you* to both of them. Then he shouted over his shoulder, "Those men are heroes, officers!" and disappeared into the store.

Into the mic, Katie Katro was heard saying, "... police are bringing out two men in handcuffs. I'm not sure what it's about. It may—"

"They killed that maniac! They didn't do anything wrong! They saved my life!" yelled a blood-covered, middle-aged African American woman over the shoulder of the reporter.

"That's right! They're not criminals! I would be dead if it wasn't for them!" a younger, shorter, blood-covered black woman added.

Looking at the camera, Ms. Katro said, "Well now, it seems to me that two survivors may have some information on the two men that were detained by the authorities."

Turning to the women, Katie said, "Hi, ladies. Are you hurt?"

"No. It's not my blood. I helped someone else to the front of the store."

"No, me either," the younger of the two said. "I was helping people, too."

"Okay, good. What are your names?"

The older woman answered, "Donna Lee."

"Dominique Rohrer."

"And were both of you in Walmart during the attack?"

"Yes, I was."

"So was I," Dominique answered.

"Did you see those two men in the store?"

"Yes, I did."

"I didn't," answered Mrs. Rohrer.

The reporter replied, "Oh, okay. Well, I don't need anything more from you. Thank you so much for your time, Ms. Rohrer."

"You're welcome. I'm going back to help out." And Dominique was off.

Katie Katro continued her impromptu interview. "Donna, do you mind telling us what you saw?"

"No problem. I was crouching down in the next aisle directly in front of the shooter. He was coming my way, but for some reason, he paused. That's when one of the boys—I believe the one wearing the red jacket—pushed him from behind, right into the space where the aisles end.

"Then they started shooting, and the white guy fell, and the other one—I'm sure now—the one with the red vest came into view still shooting the white guy while he was on the floor. And he didn't get up after that. It was over. They saved the day."

"Well, we—"

"And the one with the jacket, he fell down when he pushed that maniac. I don't even think I was *breathing!* I thought he was a goner, but I guess not, and I'm glad for that. They're heroes."

"Thank you for your account, Donna. We'll let you get back to the rescue effort. Thank you for helping out."

"You're welcome. See ya."

"Well, there you have it. Apparently, the two men that were taken away in handcuffs actually stopped the gunman. And remember, you heard it here first.

"Next up, we'll be bringing you a live press conference from the Commissioner of the Philadelphia Police Department, but first, a few words from our sponsors... "

After the break, Katie Katro said, "Welcome back to Channel 6 ABC Action News. We are at Walmart on Delaware Avenue in South Philadelphia, the site of a horrific mass shooting. We are about to get a statement from Danielle Outlaw, the Philadelphia Police Commissioner."

Surrounded by the department's top brass and dressed in a crisp midnight blue uniform decorated with medals and gold stars, Commissioner Outlaw began by saying, "Good evening, ladies and gentlemen. Uh, we won't be fielding any questions at this time, but I'll give you all of the information that we are at liberty to share.

"As you all know, a terrible mass-shooting took place today. The alleged gunman's name is Kevin Hudak. He was 28 years old and a resident of Philadelphia. His mother actually died of a heart attack here at Walmart one year ago today. Uh, we know that her death is the primary motivation for today's rampage. The shooter was targeting African Americans in particular, because he blamed them for causing his mother's fatal cardiac event.

"Uh, as far as we know, Mr. Hudak acted alone. It is unclear as to how he was able to gain intimate knowledge of the security protocols in Walmart. Investigators are currently at his home searching his electronic devices.

"Mr. Hudak did, in fact, uh, purchase the assault rifle at this location earlier today, right before he began shooting innocent people. He brought his own ammunition to the store, as well as a silenced handgun. We found the discarded homemade silencer in the wastebasket of a restricted area. Uh, that was where the killing began.

"Mr. Hudak's threat of explosive devices proved to be untrue.

"Two patrons were able to neutralize the gunman— "

IS THAT WHO YOU TOOK OUT IN HANDCUFFS?!

"Again, we aren't fielding any questions at this time. Uh, the immediate crisis is over, but we have a huge rescue effort underway. We don't have an accurate number of fatalities yet, but even one is too many.

"And I would personally like to thank the civilians for helping the wounded and transporting them to the hospitals. We all need to lean on each other right now. I have to get back to work. Thanks guys."

Katie Katro cut in, "Well, there you have it, folks. A very dark day for the city of Philadelphia. Stay tuned. We'll be bringing you continuing coverage at six."

CHAPTER 22

*D*URING THE CHANNEL 6 commercial break, things had gotten out of control in the Walmart parking lot.

As more and more survivors caught wind of the Jackson brothers' arrest, the collective mood had changed. It went from grief to anger. There were victims literally banging on the hood of the squad car that Malik and Terrell were being held in.

They couldn't understand why their heroes were being treated like petty criminals. Where was common sense? These boys had saved hundreds of lives. They didn't do anything *wrong*.

The survivors were blocking the path of the squad car. All that it could do was blast its air horn. If the police department chose to use force on the still-bleeding victims of a mass shooting, it would be a PR nightmare. Not to mention the lawsuits that would result. How the did the *cops* become the bad guys? Hint: Lock up the *good* guys.

To Malik and Terrell, it looked like the zombie apocalypse out there.

In the dim artificial light; scores of limping, blood-crusted, disheveled figures were rocking the squad car and shouting, "Let them out! Let them out! Let them out!!"

The officer in the driver's seat—an older gentleman—said, "If it was up to me, we'd be in Ruth's Chris Steakhouse right now, my treat. From where I'm sitting, you boys saved the day."

Terrell responded, "Yeah, well, from where *I'm* sittin', it definitely don't look like it."

The officer replied, "Listen, I don't know what all you boys were into, but *I'm* sure glad y'all had a gun. Y'all stopped that maniac today. And no matter what happens, that's something that you can be proud of. And I wish y'all the best. I'm serious."

"Thanks man," Terrell answered.

"Yeah, thank you, for real," said Malik.

Outside of the car, the atmosphere was markedly different. Even more civilian vehicles were flooding the plaza; the occupants getting out and demanding the authorities to release the Jackson brothers.

Some of the survivors were collapsing, either from their injuries or exhaustion. EMTs were *begging* people to accept medical treatment.

The news reporters were having a field day—all the drama that they could ask for.

The police began to regroup and reestablish order. A lieutenant instructed about fourteen patrolmen to form a human barricade around the squad car that held Malik and Terrell.

Getting it set up was another story.

Ever so gently, each officer had to position their body between the cop car and the protesters—they were no longer considered victims at this point. It was a delicate dance, a bomb technician's ballet—a powder keg. One wrong move or inadvertent touch, and the crowd could explode.

After walking on eggshells for the better part of fifteen minutes, the agile officers finally succeeded in forming their human barricade. Step by step, inch by inch, they slowly increased the secure perimeter around the car.

About sixteen more patrolmen joined the circle, one at a time. Their round blue barricade slowly morphed into a long narrow rectangle, and the officers were able to painstakingly escort the car of the hour to the plaza's exit.

With the object of their anger now out of sight, the former mob refocused their attention and resources on the rescue effort, using their personal vehicles to transport the injured to area hospitals.

* * *

1757 FRIDAY 25 NOVEMBER 2022: *SPRINGFIELD, PA*

*T*HE MOTHER OF the Jackson brothers had no idea that her boys were heroes—or even in Walmart at all—until she got to see the news.

When Elizabeth Bridgeford finished her shower and put on some fresh clothes, she walked down her carpeted stairs, sat in her favorite chair—a brown leather recliner—and turned on the TV.

"Welcome to Channel 6 ABC Action News at Six, and I'm Brian Taff. We are continuing our coverage of the tragic mass-shooting that rocked South Philadelphia earlier today.

"At approximately 3:45p.m., a man dressed in camouflage BDUs entered a Walmart on Delaware Avenue and purchased an assault rifle. Apparently, the alleged gunman, Kevin Hudak, brought his own ammunition along, concealed in the pockets of his outfit.

"The gunman then walked into a restricted area, shooting and killing all of the employees inside. From that room, he managed to simultaneously lock all of the exits, trapping hundreds of shoppers and employees. If this was pre-pandemic, the number could have easily been in the thousands.

"The gunman began his rampage by firing wildly into crowds of people, but as the minutes wore on, he seemed to be targeting certain demographics. According to reports, he even set up safe zones inside of the store for select groups of hostages.

"The gunman bought himself some time by warning law enforcement not to interfere or else he would execute African American *babies*. Many people were injured or killed before the shooter was stopped.

"Although the exact number of casualties is still unclear, if two brave young men—one of whom was armed—didn't put their own lives on the line to bring this crisis to an end, the devastation would have been even worse.

"Once the gunman was down, the store manager recovered the special key and was able to unlock the doors, allowing the first responders to render aid and restore order.

"Police recovered two semi-automatic handguns, an AR-15 assault rifle, three loaded magazines, canisters of military-grade tear gas, a stun gun, a tactical knife, an electric shaver, flashlight, and a bulletproof *Kevlar* vest from off of the gunman's person.

"Strangely enough, the two young men who stopped the shooter were taken into custody for an undisclosed reason. Here is previously recorded footage of them being escorted out of Walmart in handcuffs, and what one survivor had to say about it... "

As the crystal-clear video of Malik and Terrell played on her TV screen, Ms. Bridgeford asked out loud, "What did they get themselves into?"

The news anchor resumed his report. "The authorities are being tight-lipped about the identities of the two men who killed Kevin Hudak, the alleged maniac behind what is being dubbed the Black Friday Massacre. We'll be back with more in a few moments. Stay tuned."

Ms. Bridgeford couldn't believe her eyes or ears. She had conflicting emotions. Elizabeth witnessed her boys being taken away in handcuffs, but the woman's testimony—Donna was her name—described Malik and Terrell as heroes.

"Maybe the cops found something on one of 'em. I don't know. I'll just have to wait 'til they call me. But if what that lady said was true, then I don't have anything to worry about. None of us do.

"My boys killed a evil racist *nut*. That lady called them heroes, and she was *there*. We're gonna be fine. The truth will come out. I'll let them know when they call me. We'll be okay." Ms. Bridgeford was talking to the walls in her living room.

CHAPTER 23

0810 FRIDAY
27 NOVEMBER 2022
SCI PHOENIX

*A*S PAROLEES, MALIK and Terrell were transported directly to the state prison in their region.

While in their cell and reclining on their respective bunk beds, Terrell said, "Man, we been in this jawn for two days. It feel like two months. But 'least Mom alright."

"Yeah, that's true... Hey, 'Rell, man, I thought like once we got out the game, everything was gonna be good. How we stop hustlin', kill a terrorist, and get locked up? And I *told* you we was goin' to jail," said a frustrated Malik.

Terrell replied, "It wasn't for no drugs, though."

"Hammers is *worse!* And they said they watched us trappin'[60] for three days! So it *is* for drugs! *And* they found eleven grand!"

"They ain't never see us actually make a *sale*, though! They saw us meetin' up wit' people; that's it. They can't prove that we was sellin' *nothin'!* All the time they was watchin' us, they ain't see no bread or no work change *hands!* They ain't got nothin' on us, Bro'."

---

[60] trappin' – selling drugs

"Is you *crazy?!* We ain't got no *jobs!* They got eleven bands *and* two hammers off us!"

"'Least they ain't find the rest of 'em. We can get rid of them jawns when we get out."

"Bro', you ain't listenin'. They *got* us. We ain't *gettin'* out. We should've just flushed the rest of the work and tossed the hammers and quit cold turkey. We ain't even need the extra bread."

"C'mon, man. I was just tryin' to move the last of it and be done. And yeah Mom said, 'Don't get greedy,' but hindsight 20-20. This where we—"

"Yo, the intercom," Malik said, referring to the in-cell microphone near the door.

Terrell caught what his brother was saying and remarked, "Oh, yeah. We trippin'. Wet some toilet paper and cover it up."

Since Malik was on the bottom bunk, he was tasked with the job.

Terrell continued, "Man, this jawn ain't nothin' like Graterford. This like them jails that be on TV. All super-high security and all that for nothin'."

"'Least it got real heat. At the 'Ford, you had to *hope* your radiator was workin'. And you *still* had to put plastic over your window."

"But you could make moves in that jawn. It was wide open. You see how they treatin' us in *here?!*"

"Yeah, well, I ain't tryin' to be in none of these jawns. D.A. tryin' to charge us up. For *what*, like? We put *ourself* in danger. We could've rolled out, but we stayed to see what we could do and *this* how she treat us?!"

"I know, Bro'. And listen, if she don't drop the charges we ain't takin' no deal. We goin' to trial. We—"

"Yo, you think we should get different lawyers?"

"Naw. We gonna waive our right to separate counsel. It look better if we together: The two brothers that put they life on the line. We goin' to trial. We need this jawn on TV. We need the public involved. They sayin' that we heroes. Look how the guards in *here* treatin' us. That's what we need."

"Absolutely. The D.A. ain't just sweepin' *us* under the rug. We ain't even do nothin' wrong. She should be callin' us heroes, too. But she treatin' us like criminals."

Terrell said, "About that, right; I don't really know what's gonna happen, but I ain't got no regrets about downin' bouh. *Somebody* had to take him out. When I heard him talkin' on them loudspeakers, I *knew* he was cooked. He was *all* the way gone. That jawn was like a movie in there."

"Facts. And I wish I ain't get caught wit' that burner, but I'm still glad I had it, though. He would've killed *everybody* in that jawn; at least *way* more than he did."

"I know... 'Lik, you should've *seen* how he was creepin' down that aisle 'fore I pushed him. He was stalkin' like a animal. It's like he was huntin' us. I'm tellin' you, fam', bouh was pure evil. We definitely did the right thing."

"Well, it's all on the table now. It is what it is. But no matter what, I ain't goin' back to the streets."

"Oh yeah, ain't no doubt. That ain't even crossin' my mind. I mean, yeah, the *money* gonna be different, but... I ain't really worried 'bout that. I'm *ready* for somethin' new now. It's a little scary thinkin' 'bout goin' all the way legit, but I know it's worth it, though. Compared to *this?!* I *know* it's worth it. And then Juan? I hope he ain't *serious* like. If he send somebody at us in here, we ain't *never* gettin' out. 'Cause I ain't lettin' nobody just *kill* me."

"Yeah, I feel you. But I ain't never heard about no cartel bouhs being heavy in the PA jails. I know they up here but not in the jails like that. We ain't gotta worry 'bout nothin'."

"Yeah, well, we still gotta be on point. And say we *do* get out, we *still* gotta deal wit' bouh if he still tippin' out there. I ain't goin' through all this just to get rocked[61] *anyway*." Terrell let out an audible breath and continued speaking. "But I *definitely* don't wanna pick up another pistol neither, though. Somethin' gotta give, Bro'. I'm tired. I just wanna start *livin'* once all this over wit', man."

"I know. We gonna get there. And I told you, change ain't *never*

---

[61] rocked - killed

easy."

"Heard that."

CHAPTER 24

0930 FRIDAY
27 NOVEMBER 2022
MIFFLIN STREET

*T*HIS IS CHANNEL 3 CBS News Sunday Morning, and I'm Ukee Washington. We're live at the home of Russell Spells—the man with the green hat—who was seen escorting scores of wounded people to safety, in what's now called the Black Friday Massacre. Russell, can you tell us what you were thinking when you heard gunfire?"

Russell answered, "When the shootin' broke out, I wasn't that far away, maybe a few aisles over, so I knew it was a gun. My first thought was to pray—for me and everybody else. I just wanted to make it home in one piece. But then, when I was hidin' in a aisle wit' like fifty or sixty other people—a lot of women and kids—I started gettin' mad. I was thinkin' of like a thousand different ways I could try to stop whoever was shootin'."

"*Did* you try anything?"

"Naw. I guess common sense kicked in. I ain't have no weapons, and I ain't a violent person no more, *anyway*. I would've tried to tackle him and hold him down or somethin', and probably got shot. This ain't the movies."

"Wait. Was there a time when you *were* violent?"

"Unfortunately, yeah. And I did time in prison because of it. But

I started readin' the Bible and believin' it. And Yahweh changed my life. I repented and accepted His Son as my Savior, and I ain't been violent since."

"Good for you. So, how were you able to help so many people?"

"I was kind of followin' the shooter. Every time he left from somewhere, that's where I went. I knew I would find injured people there, so I just tried to take 'em somewhere out the way. But right before the end, when I was tryin' to get to another section, the shooter was actually comin' my way. He was in the next aisle up from me, and I froze up for a minute. But I was already helpin' somebody who leg was bleedin' real bad, so I *had* to finish the job. I couldn't just let him bleed out. I was hopin' that the shooter ain't pay me no mind."

"*Did* he notice you?"

"The Jackson brothers took him out about ten yards away from me, so he never really got the chance."

"People are calling the man with the green hat a hero. How does that make you feel?"

"I ain't no hero. I'm just a helper. Once the shooter was stopped, we was *all* helpin' the wounded. The two *Jackson* brothers the heroes, but they in prison. That don't even make no sense. They ain't no different than John Rohrer. Matter of fact, what they did is *more* commendable, 'cause they ain't have no formal training and John *did*," Russell said, recalling an incident that happened at the beginning of the year.

* * *

0900 SUNDAY 2 JANUARY 2022: *MUMMER'S PARADE*

"C'MON LET'S STAND on Washington Avenue so we can get a good spot," the young woman said.

"Isn't the window good enough?" her athletic blonde-haired husband asked.

"John Rohrer!"

"I'm playing, honey. But you *are* lucky that we live on Broad Street. Traffic is a nightmare."

At 9a.m., the sidewalks were already crowded. As John and his new bride pressed their way through the mass of people, there were only two things on his mind—protecting his wife from drunken gropers, and hoping that no one felt his gun as he brushed past them.

"See? This spot is perfect!" said an enthusiastic Dominique Rohrer, as she grabbed her husband's arm and dragged him over to a police barricade near the curb.

"That's 'cause *you're* here."

"*John*," his wife said, drawing out his name. "You are so sweet."

"Happy wife, happy life."

"And don't you forget it."

SILLY STRING! TRUMPETS! GLOW STICKS! BALLOONS!

A scruffy-looking street vendor in a green reflective vest and dirty jeans shouted out the names of his goods as he walked by—pushing a squeaking shopping cart pilfered from who knows where.

"How romantic," John quipped.

"Shut up, Babe. This is fun," Dominique said, elbowing her husband in the ribs.

"If you say—"

Just then, the String Bands fired up and began strutting their stuff. The onlookers cheered and danced and drank some more. Organized chaos. South Broad Street during the Mummer's Parade.

For some reason, John's wife couldn't stop glancing at what had to be the darkest man that she had ever seen. She was a proud black woman, but he was *black*.

The man caught her stealing a look, and he flashed what had to be the absolute whitest set of teeth that she'd ever seen. Embarrassed about getting caught, Dominique tried to focus on the parade like her husband was doing.

A few minutes later, out of the corner of her eye, Mrs. Rohrer saw the dark man pull what appeared to be a small toy machine gun from his tan three-quarter-length coat, and she whispered, "Babe, is that *real?*"

John turned to see what his wife was talking about, but before he could even respond, his fingers were wrapping around the rubber grips of his Ruger P94 lodged in a holster at the small of his back. Years of tactical training and close-quarters combat took over his body. The gun practically drew itself.

The dark man raised his carbine and shouted, "Allahu Ak—"

John pulled the trigger.

A bullet punched through the man's dark flesh, just above his left eyebrow.

Crimson droplets flew through the air like confetti.

It had sounded like one huge blast.

But two bodies dropped.

Then the screams began.

With people jumping the barricades and scattering in all directions, it was hard to see what had happened.

Fear and panic permeated the air.

And John's wife lay on the ground.

Bleeding.

* * *

1106 SUNDAY 2 JANUARY 2022: *BALA CYNWYD*

"WELCOME BACK TO NBC10 News at Eleven, and I'm Keith Jones. Meteorologist Krystal Klei will be showing you the predicted path of the Nor'easter in a few moments, but the big story on NBC10 actually happened earlier this morning. After a one-year hiatus due to the pandemic, the Mummer's Parade has finally returned—albeit a day late and not without drama.

"At approximately 9:20a.m., near the intersection of Broad Street and Washington Avenue in South Philadelphia, a Boko-Haram inspired gunman attempted to slaughter masses of attendees at the parade.

"The shooter, Omar Magondu, had a compact AR-15-style *pistol* and four extra magazines, each containing 30 rounds of ammunition. He acted alone. There were two casualties in total, but only the attacker died. The lone surviving victim was a twenty-six-year-old woman.

"Fortunately, a real-life hero managed to stop the Sudanese National before he was able to inflict massive damage on the crowd of people.

"Thirty-two-year-old John Rohrer, a Philly native and Army vet who did three tours in Afghanistan as a medic, was tipped off by his wife literally milliseconds before the gunman squeezed the trigger.

"Mr. Rohrer, who has a concealed weapons permit, drew his own firearm and shot the would-be mass-shooter in the forehead, killing him instantly. Nearby police officers quickly got the situation under control, and the Mummer's marched on.

"This story is a little bittersweet because the one person that the attacker managed to shoot was John's wife. She is currently recovering at UPenn Hospital where Mr. Rohrer works as a phlebotomist. Thankfully, her injuries weren't fatal. Mrs. Rohrer is expected to be released tomorrow.

"John Rohrer wasn't immediately available for comment, but later my colleague was able to interview the hero via Zoom."

The quality of the transmission was excellent.

"Hi, John. I'm Rosemary Connors from NBC10 News."

"Hi, Rosemary."

"I am honored to be speaking to a hero. How is your wife doing?"

"Well, the bullet passed through her side, so it didn't hit anything vital, although she would say that everything on her body is vital." They both laughed, and John continued. "She's doing fine; just in some pain, but I look forward to pampering her at our home tomorrow."

"Tell us, what was going through your mind when you saw someone pointing an actual gun in your direction?"

"I know that it would've seemed heroic or romantic for me to have been thinking about protecting my wife or all of those children and families out there, but that wasn't the case at all. To be honest, the only thing that flashed through my mind was the word *threat*.

And my combat training automatically kicked in due to the time that I spent in the military. It's that simple."

"Well, it was *still* heroic. But, why did you bring a gun to the Mummer's Parade in the first place?"

"Something told me to just take my firearm with me. I actually tried to get my wife to watch the parade form our window, but she wouldn't go for it. Since last year's was cancelled, she couldn't *wait* for this one."

"Well, John, maybe she'll take you up on that offer next year?"

"I wouldn't count on it. That little lady is fearless!"

There was more laughter, and Rosemary concluded the interview, saying, "We know that you need to get back to your wife, so let us thank you one more time for being a hero and saving the day for so many people."

"You're welcome, but my wife's the real hero. I was hypnotized by the fancy costumes. If she wouldn't have alerted me, then a lot more innocent people would have gotten hurt."

"Indeed, John. Give your wife our best."

"Will do. Take care."

* * *

0933 SUNDAY 27 NOVEMBER 2022: *MIFFLIN STREET*

"... *B*UT I'M NOT tryin' to compare 'em. I tip my hat to *all* of 'em. I'm just sayin' that somebody should be interviewin' the two courageous men who put their lives on the line on *Friday*. They the heroes, not me, but they sittin' in jail. The system can't cut 'em a break this time?

"They need to have a chance to tell they *own* story to the public. The bare facts rarely ever show the whole picture. Everybody got a past, or at least somethin' that they regret doin' in they past. People change, though."

"You obviously have some very strong feelings about the Jackson brothers' arrest."

"Absolutely. They my heroes. They saved *my* life. And I just think that they should be recognized."

"Well, Mr. Spells, I would like to thank you for your honesty. And I would like to thank you helping save lives on Black Friday."

"No problem. I'm just grateful that I was I n a position to help."

"One last question: Where's the green hat?"

"Oh, it got some blood on it, so I'ma have to get another one, even though my wife can't stand it."

"Well, we'll all be waiting to see you in it during our travels. The man with the green hat. Take care."

"You, too. Thank you."

CHAPTER 25

1131 MONDAY
5 DECEMBER 2022
CENTER CITY

*O*UTSIDE OF THE Criminal Justice Center at 13th and Filbert streets, Philadelphia's hard-nosed district attorney decided to address the public.

The city was outraged over the arrest of the Jackson brothers and what were perceived to be trumped-up charges. Supporters for the young men showed up in droves. They blanketed the streets and sidewalks. Traffic around the building was at a standstill.

In attendance were survivors of the Black Friday Massacre, the CEO of Walmart, local celebrities, professional sports team owners, half of the residents of South Philly, and high school students from all over. Even the driver of the squad car that took the boys into custody had shown up on their behalf. But he was dressed in civilian clothes.

Still, *every* body counted.

One man in attendance was standing on a trashcan, wearing a neon green hat and holding a huge poster in his hands that read:

These 2 MEN need to be judged on who they are TODAY! Who hasn't made a mistake? Malik & Terrell are SELFLESS

COURAGOUES HEROES! They stopped a TERRORIST from hurting one more human being!

The television cameras zoomed in on the face of each notable in the crowd and flashed their names at the bottom of the screen, in order to show the amount of support that the Jackson brothers had.

It seemed like the "neutral" news media was actually on their side.

Dressed in black slacks, white blouse, and unzipped black parka with fur-lined hood, Amanda Kolwitz—the Philadelphia D.A.— addressed the masses. "Good morning. I would like to begin by saying that the Philadelphia District Attorney's Office doesn't have it out for Terrell Jackson or Malik Jackson."

THEN LET THEM GO!

LET THEM GO! LET THEM GO!

"We are simply performing our civic duties according to the laws of the land. I didn't put the two young men in prison."

YES YOU DID!

"They were found with illegal firearms while on parole. That's standard procedure. I had nothing to do with that."

BOO! BOO!

"Furthermore, the charges levied against the Jackson brothers could have been far worse, but the District Attorney's Office acknowledges the fact that they stopped—"

LIAR!

"—they stopped a dangerous man from inflicting more harm on an innocent group of people. However, their act in no way justifies or nullifies their blatant disregard for the law up *to* that point."

BOO! BOO!

LOSER!

"I would be doing this fine city a disservice if I allowed felons on parole to run wild—"

YOU'RE A FELON!

BOO!

"—to run wild with no consequences for their actions. I am

confident that the criminal justice system will determine the appropriate outcomes for Terrell and Malik Jackson."

LET THEM GO! LET THEM GO!

YOU SUCK!

"Seeing that this is an active case, I will not be fielding any questions at this time. Thank you very much."

And with that, the Philadelphia District Attorney concluded her address and proceeded to leave.

BOO!

YOU SUCK!

WE HATE YOU!

Amanda Kolwitz stopped mid-stride, turned around, and walked back up to the podium, saying, "See? This is the *exact* attitude that threatens our democracy. You *hate* me? Why? Because I won't do what you want me to do?"

YEAH THAT'S WHY!

YEAH!

"It's *that* sense of entitlement that's teaching this generation *not* to be accountable for their actions. You see it on college campuses, in Hollywood, in professional sports, in the music industry, in the corporate world—"

BOO!

"Know what? Forget it."

GET OUT OF HERE!

GO HOME!

I STILL HATE YOU!

As Ms. Kolwitz retreated back into the CJC, the crowd erupted into cheers, and they began chanting, "Let them go! Let them go! Let them go!"

* * *

1217 MONDAY 5 DECEMBER 2022: *LOCUST STREET*

*H*AVING FINALLY MADE it back to his truck, Russell felt sickened. Nothing about the district attorney's public address was encouraging. He stuck his key in the ignition but didn't turn it. *Man, it ain't lookin' good.* He felt like screaming.

Russell exhaled, gave the top of his steering wheel two whacks with the palm of his gloved hand, and prayed out loud. "Yahweh, that lady ain't *right!* She gonna try to *bury* them bouhs!

"You know the charges they got, but that ain't right, though. They ain't monsters. I was *there*. *Please* help 'em. *Some* kind of way." He sighed, then continued, "In my savior Yahshua's name I ask You this. Thank You, Dad."

Russell turned the key, started up his truck, and drove off.

* * *

0945 TUESDAY 10 JANUARY 2023: *CRIMINAL JUSTICE CENTER*
MALIK AND TERRELL were waiting in the holding pen, wearing fluorescent orange jumpsuits with the letters *D.O.C.* printed on their backs.

Finally, their lawyer called for them. They were escorted to yet another room, and their counsel was waiting at a table.

When the Jackson boys walked in, the always-dapper Frank Gallo said, "Morning gentlemen. I already know where you stand, but the D.A. is willing to drop the Voluntary Manslaughter and Conspiracy to Commit Voluntary Manslaughter charges, as well as the Drug Trafficking charge, if you both plead out to Possession of Illegal Firearm and Reckless Endangerment. And they will also recommend that the Pennsylvania Board of Probation and Parole not take your street time or max out your current sentences, *if* you agree to the deal."

Malik replied, "Man, that ain't no deal! They ain't catch us *sellin'* no drugs! The D.A. can *have* the money they found. We ain't coppin' no plea. She gonna *roof* us on the gun charges. And the Board don't care what *nobody* say; they do what they want. We takin' it to trial. We goin' all the way."

"I'll let them know your decision. And I'll keep preparing. I'll talk with you guys soon. Do you want me to update your mother?"

Terrell told him, "Naw, we got it. Thanks. Just get all the witnesses you can."

"That won't be a problem. Take care."

* * *

*T*HE MAROON MERCURY Marauder had two blocks to go before it reached its destination. One right turn. Drive a block and a half. Make a left. Paydirt.

Juan—in a rush to collect twenty-two grand and offload some of Mexico's unofficial number one export—caught the yellow light but forgot to use his turn signal.

Officer Erin Walker—great granddaughter of legendary beat cop Seamus MacGregor Walker—was waiting at the intersection behind a beige Mini Cooper and didn't miss a thing. When her light turned green, the Mini turned left, she turned on her red-and-blues, and stomped down on the accelerator. The patrol car flew up behind the bombed-out[62] Mercury, and Officer Walker blipped her siren.

Juan couldn't believe his bad luck. First, his favorite girlfriend gets killed at Walmart; he told her to call out sick that day. Then, two of his best customers—the famous Jackson brothers—get locked up. He was looking forward to shooting them in their faces for their disloyalty and disrespect. And for not saving his associate-manager girlfriend. Fake heroes. Planting them in the dirt would have eased his pain. And now, he's getting pulled over—at the *wrong time.*

"Everything okay. All I do is be calm." The bronze-skinned Mexican with the cruiserweight frame always spoke English to himself when he was nervous.

The Mercury made a left turn and pulled into the parking lot of a crowded shopping center. Juan drove to an open area and put his car in *Park*.

Officer Walker was right on his bumper, spotlight beaming on his

---

[62] bombed-out – heavily tinted

back window, red-and-blues still blazing. She radioed in the traffic stop, exited her vehicle, and approached the left side of the Marauder.

Hand on her service weapon.

The strap on the holster undone.

Juan already had his window down in spite of the cold. No need to complicate things.

"License, registration, insurance." More of a demand than a request. Officer Walker wanted to assert her authority early.

Juan asked, "Can you tell me what I do, Officer?"

"You didn't use your turn signal back there. License, regis—"

Juan handed over his credentials.

Officer Walker then said, "Thank you. Do you mind turning the car off and handing me the keys?"

Juan went from zero to sixty in a split second. "What for, Officer?! I give you what you ask for! My paper good!"

"Sir, calm down and shut off the vehicle. *Now!*"

The heated exchange drew Officer Walker a bit closer toward the front of the Mercury than she should have been. She was positioned at the center of the driver's door, although she was trained to stand parallel with the B-pillar—just behind a driver's shoulder.

There's a reason for everything.

As Juan's right hand was reaching for the ignition, his left hand came up from his lap with a 9mm Walther PPK. He had it tucked underneath his thigh. Standard procedure anytime that he went to do a deal.

The officer was too concerned with the ignition getting switched off to notice the chrome pistol that the driver was aiming at her torso.

Mistake number two.

Without warning, the Walther flashed and thundered.

Walker instinctively pushed off with her left foot to pivot away from the barrage of bullets and simultaneously pulled her standard-issue Glock 17 as she fell to the ground.

Juan went to make his escape, but in his haste to get away, he forgot to put his foot on the brake before attempting to shift out of *Park.*

Officer Walker emptied her clip into the driver's side of the Marauder, striking Juan in the left hip, left thigh, left elbow, left triceps, left shoulder, left ear, and finally the head as he tried to duck down and put the car into gear.

His body slumped.

The horn let out one long continuous blast.

Game over.

And then Erin lost consciousness.

* * *

1820 TUESDAY 10 JANUARY 2023: *SCI PHOENIX*

*T*HE JACKSON BROTHERS were hanging out in the dayroom of their housing unit. Malik was sitting at a table watching the big TV on the wall, and Terrell was playing Spades with three other PVs[63] from South Philly.

Yet another 'Breaking News' notification flashed across the screen during the broadcast.

Sharrie Williams from Channel 6 ABC Action News was heard saying, "... officer-involved shooting occurred at approximately 5:50p.m. at the Leo Mall just off of Byberry Road in the Somerton section of Philadelphia.

"In what appeared to be a routine traffic stop, the driver of the vehicle pulled into a busy shopping center. After handing the police officer his credentials, some kind of a debate ensued, and the driver fired on the female officer, striking her several times in the abdomen. She returned fire, killing the operator of the vehicle; he was the only occupant.

"Thankfully, the police officer was wearing her body armor. The initial prognosis was a few cracked ribs. The patrolwoman is expected to make a full recovery. We are not able to disclose any other details at this time, as the incident is currently under investigation. However, we do have footage of the alleged gunman's bullet-riddled car... "

Malik couldn't believe his eyes. "Hey, 'Rell! Look at the TV! Hurry

---

[63] PVs – Parole Violators

up! Juan got in a shootout wit' the cops! That's his car! Look, that's where we met him at before!"

Terrell looked up at the flatscreen, then he excused himself from the card game and hurried over to his brother. In a low voice he said, "Yo, that's really him, 'Lik! That's his *car!* That's *crazy!*"

"I know, right? I can't even believe it. 'Least that's one hurdle out the way, though."

Realizing the gravity of the incident, Terrell sighed. "Yeah... But that *is* messed up, though. Bouh *dead.*"

"What you mean?! He would've done the same thing to *us!*"

"Maybe, maybe not. But it ain't no comin' back from that, man. I mean, yeah. It's one less thing to worry about, but dude really *dead* like. *Yeah* we fell out, but we knew bouh for *years*, though. He part of the reason why we up. And *I* know it was only about the money— we was coppin' *heavy*. But I ain't happy he *dead*, though. I mean, yeah, if he would've came at us, we would've had to put him down, but he was our partner, though. That ain't nothin' to celebrate."

"I ain't celebratin' him *dyin'*, Bro'. I'm just sayin' we ain't gotta be worryin' 'bout *when* he comin', *how* he comin', if we could get to a *burner* in time. That's what *I'm* sayin'—one less thing on our plate. I'm fightin' for my *life* in here. D.A. tryin' to kill me. *He* wanted to kill me. Now he can't. I ain't wrong."

"I don't know. I guess all this stuff just changin' me. I feel like I'm *over* the streets now. I don't want no more, 'Lik. I'm *cool*. I just wanna live, man. And it's crazy, 'cause even though I ain't feelin' no type of way[64] about the Man-Man situation no more, I really don't even wanna *give* him no line.[65] I don't want nothin' to do wit' *nothin'*. If I push him deeper in the game, I'm just keepin' the cycle goin'. I can't do that, man. I just want all this stuff to end. Get this case over wit' one way or another and just live. They could *have* the streets."

"I feel you, Bro'. And we ain't got no excuses now. How*ever* this

---

[64] feelin' no type of way – not upset

[65] line – connect a.k.a. drug wholesaler

trial go, we all the way out."

"We all the way out," echoed Terrell.

The elder Jackson gave his codefendant a shoulder hug and walked back to the card table.

CHAPTER 26

*T*HE WHITE-HAIRED, white-bearded, black-robed judge asked, "Would the defense like to give a closing statement?"

Decked out in an expensive gray Savile Row suit and leather-soled loafers, Frank Gallo, the chief counsel for the Jackson brothers, responded, "Yes. Thank you, your honor."

Turning to the racially diverse jury, the criminal defense attorney began. "Jurors, fellow *Philadelphians*, my clients—my *heroes*— Malik Jackson and Terrell Jackson are not on trial for, they are *not* being prosecuted for a criminal act. These two courageous, unselfish brothers are facing decades behind bars for confronting a monster and saving the lives of hundreds of strangers. *That's* why you're here today; to determine if you should lock away these two young men for protecting your community. They may have even saved some of *your* friends or family members on the day in question. But you're going to be instructed by the prosecution to find the Jackson brothers guilty of manslaughter. Where's the justice in that?"

Meeting the gaze of each juror, Frank Gallo would pace back and forth and abruptly stop as he drove his points home. For dramatic effect. Throughout his discourse, any one of the twelve jurors could be seen nodding in agreement.

Mr. Gallo continued, "Did they kill a man? Yes. But *who* did they kill, and *why?* Kevin Hudak, a hate-filled, raging maniac with no regard for human life. That's the *who.* The *why? Why* did Malik and Terrell kill an active-shooter, a mass-murderer? *Why?* No. The question should be: Why did these two brothers put their *lives* on the line for people that they didn't even know? I'll tell you why. Change.

"Malik and Terrell—of their own volition—decided to change their lives well before they were taken into custody by the police. And they were *actively* taking the steps to do so. On trial are not two hardened criminals—as the prosecution wants you to believe. On trial are two changed men—*brothers*—who laid it all on the line for the benefit of someone else.

"Now, it's public record that Malik and Terrell have made some mistakes in life. Who hasn't? *Who* is perfect? None of us. But not all of us can honestly say that we would have done the same. Not all of us can say that we would have put strangers before ourselves. Not all of us can say that and mean it. But the Jackson brothers don't have to say a thing. Their *actions*, on that fateful blackest of Fridays, spoke volumes.

"The prosecution is going to tell you that you've heard the facts and seen the evidence; but *context* is everything. And this is *not* the context for condemnation! These heroes need to be celebrated. Or at the very least, acquitted.

"If society ever allows the selfless act of saving lives to be second-guessed because of the possible ramifications, then we're *all* going to be in trouble. Today, we have a chance to prevent that. Today, we can reinforce the fact that it's okay to put others before ourselves. *Today*, we can come to the rescue for someone else.

"My fellow Philadelphians, please don't penalize these two young men for doing the *right* thing." Frank Gallo paused for a beat to let his plea sink in, then he closed. "I appreciate your time." The lawyer tapped the jury box's railing with his fingertips, turned to the judge and said, "The defense rests, your honor."

The honorable Father Time looked at the D.A., saying, "I

presume that the state would like to give a rebuttal to the defense's closing argument?"

"Yes, your honor," the D.A. answered as she stood up.

Amanda Kolwitz walked over to the twelve men and women seated to her left and said, "People of the jury, it's up to YOU, now. The fates of Malik and Terrell Jackson are in YOUR hands. YOU, juror, are responsible for ensuring the public's safety—YOUR community's safety. Ask yourself: Would releasing these two felons make MY community safer?

"Yes, these two men stopped a mass-shooter. Yes, they risked their lives. Yes—as far as the defense is concerned—it was an unselfish act.

"But was a felon armed with an illegal gun? Yes. Did a felon fire that unlawful weapon in a crowded store? Yes. Was another illegal firearm found in the vehicle being used by the two felons? Yes.

"Were eleven thousand American dollars found in their possession? Yes. Were they frequently meeting with known drug dealers? Yes. Were these drugs poisoning our communities? Yes.

"Were these two brazen men consistently disregarding the laws of the land *and* the stipulations of their respective parole terms? Yes and yes.

"Simply because of this *one* good deed, would YOU give these two convicted felons—hardened criminals—a free pass, even after they have demonstrated time and time again that they are *not* going to change?

"Or will YOU let the laws of the land, put into place by the officials that YOU elected, determine the appropriate fates for these two gun-slinging, drug-pushing felons?

"Guilty or not guilty? Hero or *criminal?* I hope that YOU will make the responsible choice."

*T*ELEVISION CAMERAS WEREN'T allowed inside of the courtroom, but outside was another story.

"This is FOX 29 News. I'm Alex Holley."

"And I'm Mike Jerrick."

Alex continued, "And we are live outside of the Criminal Justice Center in downtown Philadelphia, awaiting the verdict in the Jackson brothers' trial. Today was the final day for closing arguments, and the jury has already begun deliberating in this high-profile, high-stakes case.

"The two men on trial, Malik Jackson and Terrell Jackson, were on state parole and in possession of illegal firearms when they stopped a crazed gunman in Walmart last November.

"The brothers are charged with Voluntary Manslaughter, Conspiracy to Commit Voluntary Manslaughter, Drug Trafficking, Possession of Illegal Firearms, and Reckless Endangerment. Naturally, they are hoping for a *Not Guilty* verdict due to their unselfish deed.

"I apologize for having to raise my voice, but as you can see, it is jam-packed around this courthouse. Traffic has been rerouted, and Philadelphia's finest are standing by in case things get out of hand."

Mike cut in, saying, "Yeah, supporters for the Jackson brothers have shown up by the *ton*. The public are hailing these men as heroes. And a lot of the people are wearing *Free the Jacksons* T-shirts on this hot June day.

"You can actually feel the tension in the air. With the recent string of unrelated protests, we have no idea how the public will react if the Jackson brothers are found guilty.

"To complicate the situation—should violence break out—there is a large number of *teenagers* here in support of Malik and Terrell. The last day of school is tomorrow, but the students want to start their summer vacation off with something to talk about. Hopefully not anything too extreme.

"Alex, what do you think will happen in the courtroom today?"

She answered, "It is highly unlikely that the Jackson brothers will be acquitted, because of the overwhelming physical and video evidence against them. A guilty verdict would mean that Malik and Terrell are sent back to their cell at SCI Phoenix, where they would have to finish out their current prison sentences, and then serve an additional number of years when they are sentenced on their new case. That's *only* if the brothers are found guilty."

Mike interjected, "I don't know if I'm allowed to say this, but I hope the day goes in their favor. That D.A. is out for blood. There are always a miserable few who just don't believe that people can change. Malik and Terrell saved a lot of lives, and I commend them. But it's entirely up to the jury. And that's not a *bad* thing. Unless those jurors were living in a bubble since last November, it's *impossible* for them not to have heard all of the positive eyewitness testimony and public support for the Jackson brothers. I don't care *who* you are; that'll leave an impression on you."

Mr. Jerrick glanced at his colleague and she took over. "Were the Jackson brothers thugs, simply concerned with self-preservation? Or were they truly heroes, rising up to meet the occasion? Only time will tell.

"We have several supporters lined up who are waiting to share their thoughts. We'll be bringing them to you live, right after the break. But real quick, before we go, answer this question: If you were on the jury, what would *you* do?

"Stay with us."

CHAPTER 27

*T*HE COURTROOM WAS abuzz with subdued conversation as the stakeholders and general attendees anticipated the jury's decision. The spectators were prepared to stick it out until the conclusion of the business day if need be. No one wanted to leave the room prematurely. This was history in the making.

The Philadelphia Sheriff's Office occupied a substantial portion of real estate in the wood-adorned legal venue. They weren't taking any chances. Riots have broken out over less. But hopefully not today. Not if they could help it. There was too much at stake. So they remained vigilant. Watching. Waiting.

Suddenly, the solid walnut door creaked open, and a hush fell over the crowd. Everyone was ordered to stand while the jurors filed back into the courtroom. Once the twelve men and women had taken their places, the throng of bodies were permitted to sit down again.

Father Time looked to his right and said, "Madame Floor-person, please hand me the verdict," and he took a moment to look it over. When he handed it back, he said, "Please render your verdict."

Terrell's and Malik's eyes were fixated on the pretty floor-person. But not because of her beauty. That was the furthest thing from their minds. All that the Jackson brothers cared about was what she had to say.

The young woman tucked some loose strands of hair behind her right ear and said, "We, the people of the jury, for the charge of *Drug Trafficking*, find the defendants Malik Jackson and Terrell Jackson not guilty. For the charge of *Reckless Endangerment*, we find the defendants not guilty. For the charge of *Possession of Illegal Firearm*, we find the defendants not guilty. For the charge of *Voluntary Manslaughter*, we find the defendants not gui—"

WHOO!

YEAH!

The Jackson brothers' supporters could no longer contain themselves. They would've been at home in any sports arena in the country.

The judge repeatedly banged his gavel and trumpeted, "Order in the court! Order in my courtroom! I'll charge you all with contempt! There is one more charge to be heard! Quiet down! Settle down."

The revelers grudgingly obliged.

The judge turned to the young woman and said, "Please continue."

Madame Floor-person gave one curt nod of her head and said, "Finally, for the charge of *Conspiracy to Commit Voluntary Manslaughter*, we, the people of the jury, find the defendants Malik Jackson and Terrell Jackson not guilty."

Amid a cacophony of cheers, Father Time said, "I accept your verdicts. Your duty in this courtroom is complete."

While their fate was being played out before their eyes, the Jackson brothers wore poker faces; but after the last verdict was pronounced, Terrell and Malik simultaneously exhaled and looked at one another with huge smiles on their faces and leaned over and hugged right from their chairs.

Then two sheriff's deputies approached them.

In the meantime, the team of defense attorneys were backslapping and high-fiving each other. The spectators were cheering like when the Eagles won the Superbowl.

Even the many people—and some police officers—lining the walls of the hallway outside of the courtroom started cheering when they heard the celebration coming from the other side of the door.

Seemingly every news outlet in the state was represented, and their reporters and camera operators were ready—microphones in hand for the former; for the latter, lenses pointed directly at the double-doors of the courtroom.

As expected, the state's attorneys came out first. A woman dressed head to toe in red led the way. The reporters were all over her.

MRS. KOLWITZ, DO YOU HAVE ANYTHING TO SAY ABOUT WHAT HAPPENED IN THERE?

DO YOU THINK THAT JUSTICE WAS SERVED TODAY?

Without breaking her stride, Amanda Kolwitz dejectedly mumbled, "No comment."

She couldn't get to her office fast enough. not fast enough at all. Philadelphia had no shortage of hecklers in attendance.

BOO!

AH-HA! YOU LOST!

THAT'S WHAT YOU GET!

LOSER!

THANKS FOR WASTING MY TAX DOLLARS!

I STILL HATE YOU!

No sooner did the insults cease, than the Jackson brothers get taken out of the courtroom in handcuffs. This was the moment the media had been waiting for. Too bad that their questions couldn't be heard over the ear-splitting shouts and whistles. As they were marched off under police escort, Terrell and Malik shouted *Thank Yous* all the way down the hall and onto the waiting elevator.

Everything was fine. Just about *everyone* knew that the Jackson brothers had to go back to SCI Phoenix and wait to be released by the parole board. Stupid bureaucracy. But it didn't take too long. Just a couple of weeks. In *this* case.

CHAPTER 28

*A*FTER THEIR RELEASE, Terrell and Malik kept the promise that they made to themselves. No more drugs. No more guns. Crime was no longer an option.

The mayor of Philadelphia held a barbecue on the west apron of City Hall, honoring the Jackson brothers, hailing them as true heroes. Many of the survivors showed up; and those who couldn't make it, they sent cards or gifts.

The "Bedding Aisle Survivors" shared their personal accounts of the final moments of that fateful Black Friday, and when they expressed their heartfelt gratitude for Malik and Terrell stopping the shooter just in the nick of time, the Jackson brothers could no longer hold back the tears.

They were heroes.

And they were free.

From everything.

Terrell and Malik were inundated with job offers from the city's elite. The day couldn't get any better.

Out of the blue, the governor of Pennsylvania showed up with a small entourage, and everyone fell silent. He approached the microphone, and when he concluded his address with the words, "... do hereby grant Terrell Jackson and Malik Jackson full pardons, effective immediately," the crowd exploded into cheers. Their shouts could be heard all the way to the Lakes![66]

The Jackson brothers were in shock.

They were never foolish enough to even *think* that they would be completely out of the system one day. No parole? No criminal record? No barriers to employment?

Their proud mother simply cried. Her boys were free.

The crowd began to chant, "Speech! Speech! Speech!"

Malik and Terrell had no choice but to comply.

Placing his can of Pepsi underneath his chair and setting his styrofoam plate on his seat, Malik J. Jackson walked to the microphone and said, "Never in my wildest dreams would I have imagined this day. Last month, I ain't know what was gonna happen in court, and now look at us. Look at us all.

"I love this city 'cause of the people who live here. We might not always greet each other, but when one of our own is in trouble, we come together. Black, white, Muslim, Christian, rich, poor—it don't matter.

"I thank all of y'all so much for supportin' me and 'Rell through all of this. *Y'all* the heroes!

"And we ain't gonna let y'all down, neither. We made a promise to *ourself* on Thursday, November 24th, 2018, that we was gettin' out the game.

"Black Friday was actually our last day—*before* all the drama started. Right before bouh went crazy, we was all the way done. We was on our way to throw our guns in the river, but we never made it out the store.

"A old friend of mine ran up to me and told me that she seen somebody wit' a gun. So me and 'Rell stuck around to see what was goin' on.

"I don't really know *why* we ain't leave, but lookin' back now, I'm

---

glad we didn't; 'cause we would've never got to meet none of y'all.

"I *know* everything happen for a reason. I ain't bitter. I ain't mad at the cops. They was just doin' they job. They did the right thing. And so did y'all, by comin' to our rescue when we needed it.

"Man, I'm just glad to *be* here. It feel so good to be *free!* I love y'all! Thank you, Governor Wolf! I'ma turn it over to my brother," concluded Malik.

The crowd applauded and cheered.

With a big smile on his face, and seven words on his heart, Terrell Jackson stepped up to the microphone and took a deep, shaky breath. He looked out over the crowd. "What *he* said. I love y'all, Philadelphia!"

EPILOGUE

*T*HE FAMILIAR SILVER Honda Accord was parked on the Southwest corner of 17th and Annin streets. The Jackson brothers were inside. Waiting.

Since it was an unseasonably warm April day, their windows were already rolled down. No need to wait 'til the last minute.

"Hey 'Lik, grab that jawn for me. It's behind your seat. Hurry up! That's Man-Man and them comin' down the block! They ain't gonna catch me empty-handed twice," Terrell told his brother.

"Here, Bro'. We got 'em *this* time." Malik handed his brother a black Samsonite briefcase. "You want me to do it?"

"Naw, I got it. This *personal*." Terrell cracked open the briefcase and pulled out several brochures to give to Man-Man and a few other young guys from the neighborhood.

It was time for the Jackson brothers to raise the village.

Terrell and Malik were living a dream. They went from carrying guns to carrying briefcases as the founders of a nonprofit organization called *What It Takes*. The CEO of Walmart even provided a huge building for the organization to facilitate its day-to-day operations. The nonprofit caters to felons and at-risk youths.

Because the Pennsylvania Department of Corrections continues to fail to adequately prepare the men for successful reentry into society, Terrell and Malik Jackson had no choice but to man-up and try to solve the problem.

In-house, *What It Takes* conducts various monthly workshops including Money Management, Resume Writing & Interview Skills, Basic Cooking, Healthier Living, Community Stewardship, and Business Education.

Additionally, the organization holds a weekly group to discuss personal struggles and to share triumphs.

What It Takes also plays the role of a middle-man, connecting its clients with companies willing to provide vocational training and job placement.

What sets their organization apart is its "Dayternship" program. *What It Takes* partners with entrepreneurs, authors, local businesses, federal corporations, hospitals, municipal agencies, schools, politicians, law enforcement, and fire departments in order to show their clients "what it takes" to enter into a specific field.

The Jackson brothers hope that their business model catches on nation-wide, with other unlikely "heroes" stepping up to the plate to save a troubled generation.

In another part of the country, a storm was brewing.

Not unaware of the fairly recent happenings in Philadelphia, a large meeting was called.

The General trumpeted, "Listen up, men! We will not let our brother's murder go unavenged! He made the ultimate sacrifice! Philadelphia Sergeant's heroic actions will reverberate throughout the annals of history! He didn't die in vain! Let his deeds be an inspiration to you all!

"In one short year, I molded him into the ultimate assassin. He had the raw material, same as you all have—heart! But Philadelphia Sergeant only had one year of long-distance training, and look what he accomplished!

"Should we do any less?! I can't hear you!"

NO!

"I said, 'Should we do any *less?!*'"

NO!

"Philadelphia Sergeant set the precedent. From now on, every single Black Friday, we're gonna make our presence felt! Store by store, mall by mall, every Black Friday is open season on darkies!"

YEAH!

"We're gonna plan, we're gonna practice, and we're gonna execute! Our goal isn't to die. Our goal is to kill and live to kill some *more!*"

YEAH!

"Step up your recruiting efforts, men. Put some feelers out there. Be a little more vocal at your work and in the chatrooms. We can have platoons in every city.

"It's a lot more like-minded people out there looking to join our cause. They just need to know that we exist. *Do* we exist?"

YEAH!

"*Are* we the best?"

YEAH!

"Are we afraid?"

NO FEAR!

"That's right! No fear! It's time for the White Knights to come out of the shadows!"

YEAH! YEAH! YEAH!

AFTERWORD

I would like to express my most sincere condolences to the families and loved ones of the victims of the August 3, 2019 mass-shooting at Walmart in El Paso, Texas. My prayers are with the survivors and all affected parties. I am truly sorry and deeply saddened.

I wrestled with releasing *Hero or Criminal* when I became aware of the tragedy in El Paso. Although I wrote this book well before any of the 2019 Walmart shootings, I didn't want it to appear as though I was trying to capitalize off of someone else's pain.

Why did I continue with publication? There were some other messages and issues in the book that I wanted to bring to light. I'd hoped that once I was released from prison, the tragic event in El Paso wouldn't be so fresh and raw in the hearts and minds of the general public.

That my fictional book may potentially spark memories of that fateful real-life morning in Texas is unsettling still. I don't want to revictimize anyone. This was one of the hardest decisions that I had to make. I pray that I made the right one.

<u>*ACKNOWLEDGMENTS*</u>

I give thanks to the heavenly Father Yahweh and His Son Yahshua. All that I have—life, family, gifts, abilities—was given to me by my Father in heaven, and I am forever grateful. I pray that my outward existence reflects my inner gratitude.

This is my first full-length work of fiction. It was an exciting journey. I was amazed to see the story take on a life of its own. I was no longer writing, but recording the events as they unfolded. I knew where I needed to go, but I had no idea how I was going to get there. The characters themselves took me to my destination.

I would like to thank Terrell Jackson, Malik Jackson, Man-Man, Tara Johannsen, Kevin Hudak, Elizabeth Bridgeford, and Russell Spells for letting me into their respective worlds and allowing me to tell their story. It was a joy getting to know them, and they'll never be forgotten.

I must thank my mother Donna Patterson for her support, fictional expertise, and helpful suggestions. She is a true gem.

Thank you, Marie & Tarik and Janine & Keith, for holding it down when I couldn't.

And thank you Jada, Basil, Lex, and Caia for forcing—I mean, motivating—me to come up with all kinds of ways to provide for you wonderful children. I wouldn't trade y'all for anything!

To my Kareen, welcome to the family. I'm so excited for you!

I gotta give a shout-out to my man Elliott "Champ" Eberhardt, a.k.a. E. Fresh, an incarcerated entrepreneur and author of *From Inmate To Boss*. He showed me the ropes in the world of fiction and traded war stories with me in the nonfiction realm.

Last but not least, much respect goes out to Mark "Mustafa" Galloway, also incarcerated, who has absolutely no idea of the role he played in the creation of *Hero or Criminal*. And he won't know until he receives this book and reads this page. (Thanks 'Staf!)

In December of 2018, we had a conversation over breakfast about all of the celebrities that were being televised feeding the needy during the holiday season. Mark contrasted their display of charity with broke-by-comparison college students working pro-bono, spending their time and money, laboring tirelessly to get prisoners exonerated. He then asked a rhetorical question: Are the college kids heroes or what?

The seed was planted, and the idea for a book was born. I planned on writing a nonfiction story about that very thing. But my imagination got the best of me, and I ended up mapping out the plot for *Hero or Criminal*. The original title was *Heroes or What?* but that didn't quite mesh with the new direction that I was taking. So that was that, and this is the result.

Thank YOU, reader. Thank YOU for reading my book. I hope that you enjoyed it. I hope that it was worth your time.